CW01509356

IF YOU WANNABE MY MARQUESS

MERRY FARMER

IF YOU WANNABE MY MARQUESS

Copyright ©2021 by Merry Farmer

This book is licensed for your personal enjoyment only. This book may not be re-sold or given away to other people. If you would like to share this book with another person, please purchase an additional copy for each recipient. If you're reading this book and did not purchase it, or it was not purchased for your use only, then please return to your digital retailer and purchase your own copy. Thank you for respecting the hard work of this author.

This book is a work of fiction. Names, characters, places, and incidents are products of the author's imagination or are used fictitiously. Any resemblance to actual events or locales or persons, living or dead, is entirely coincidental.

Cover design by Erin Dameron-Hill (the miracle-worker)

ASIN: B08V5GQ32C

Paperback ISBN: 9798717368810

Click here for a complete list of other works by Merry Farmer.

If you'd like to be the first to learn about when the next books in the series come out and more, please sign up for my newsletter here: http://eepurl.com/RQ-KX

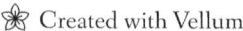 Created with Vellum

CHAPTER 1

BALLYMENA, IRELAND – SEPTEMBER, 1888

*J*t was a simple fact of nature that men considered it their purpose in life to dominate and manage women. Colleen O'Shea had seen the nefarious intentions of the male of the species play out over and over again. She'd seen it in the way the schoolmaster who had been hired to serve as tutor for her brother, Lord Fergus O'Shea, Earl of Ballymena, had fawned over Fergus and snubbed her and her sisters when all they'd wanted to do was learn. She'd noted it when the great lords of County Antrim had looked down their noses at the fine, intelligent ladies they asked to dance with at balls and soirees, as if all the ladies had to offer were shapely bosoms instead of bright minds. And she noticed it in the way Fergus had declared his intention to bully and badger all of his sisters into marriage, now that he'd returned to Ireland. He'd already managed to catch Colleen's sister, Marie, in his marriage trap— although, to be honest, Marie hadn't put up much of a fight. That had more to do with her new husband, Lord Christian Darrow, Earl of Kilrea, and his handsome face and teasing eyes, than any convincing Fergus might have done.

Colleen, however, was determined to fight her brother's meddling and the institution of marriage tooth and nail. She had no intention of falling victim to the domination that so many men still thought they were entitled to. Hadn't they read the exciting works of the progressive women who were heralding a new age of female independence? Had they never heard of the lines of Annie Besant, Emmeline Pankhurst, or Harriet McIlquham?

Fergus most likely thought his heart was in the right place as he scoured northern Ireland for men to marry his womenfolk, but as Colleen and her sisters well knew, he had committed one major mistake while attempting to appease them. In exchange for curtailing their freedom by forcing them to move from the seaside cottage, where the four of them had been residing, back into the main house of Dunegard Castle, he had given them all bicycles of the highest quality and most modern design. Said bicycles enabled the sisters to embrace their freedom rather than curtailing it.

"Are you certain it was a good idea to strap barrels of beer to the back of these things?" Colleen panted, peddling the last few yards through the back alley behind Ballymena's main street. She'd long since broken out in a sweat, and she was reasonably certain her legs wouldn't support her once they stopped in back of The Hangman Pub and dismounted to deliver their order.

"This is the perfect solution to our transportation problems," Shannon—Colleen's oldest sister—said, out of breath herself. "Since Fergus forbid us to use the cart."

"Which one of you alerted him to our ongoing commercial activities?" Marie huffed, straining to pedal the last bit of the journey to the pub.

Ahead, in the alley, Mr. Coney, the pub's owner, had stepped out of the pub and was watching the four sisters struggle forward with their loads. He wore a grin that Colleen found far too indulgent for her tastes.

"It wasn't me," Chloe—her youngest sister—said in a hurry. Chloe's face was red from exertion, and her ginger hair was plastered to her forehead with sweat.

It was likely that all four of them looked more like exhausted farmhands than the titled ladies they were. If anyone had seen the sisters of an earl loitering in the alley in back of a common pub, puffing from the effort of riding bicycles laden with barrels of beer, none of them would have withstood the scandal, regardless of what advances the likes of Emmeline Pankhurst was making for their sex.

Shannon shot a wary look to Chloe. "Perhaps it would be best if we pretended our brewing venture no longer existed at all," she said with a narrow-eyed look.

"But women have been brewers for centuries," Chloe protested as they rode up to The Hangman's back door. "It was an exclusively female endeavor all through the Middle Ages. I read about it in a history book. The book didn't even have pictures."

Marie laughed as she shifted her feet from her bicycle's pedals to the ground and leaned forward over her handlebars. "Is it only books without pictures that have authority, then?" she asked.

"I'd be surprised if you've read a book at all recently," Colleen teased her with a lopsided grin. "I'm surprised you deigned to leave your dear, delicious husband for more than a few minutes to join us."

"Christian believes it is important for a woman to have her own interests and activities, even when she is married," Marie said with a mock imperious look. She couldn't hold the look, though, and dissolved into wicked giggles. "Besides, he's a bit sore today."

Shannon rolled her eyes. Chloe blinked obliviously. Colleen knew enough to guess that Marie was talking about sexual relations, but it was beyond her why Lord Kilrea would be sore. From the gossip she'd heard, it was the lady who was far more likely to end up smarting as a result of the marriage bed.

"I'm surprised that Lord Kilrea let you out of the house at all," Colleen said, dismounting her bicycle with a groan. Fortunately, a young man from the pub joined Mr. Coney in unstrapping the barrels of beer and taking them into the pub so she didn't have to exert herself further. "I'm surprised you're able to have your own thoughts at all, seeing as you were so foolish as to fall into Fergus's marriage trap."

"Yes, Marie," Chloe added with a scolding click of her tongue. "That really was unwise of you."

"I believe our dear sister feels she's made a good bargain in trading her freedom for *other things*," Shannon said, sending Marie a downright wicked look.

Marie met that look with a teasing flicker of one eyebrow. "There are benefits to finding oneself under a man."

Colleen was certain she was speaking in some sort of double entendre, but she ignored what she didn't fully understand and shook her head. "You'll never catch me tripping up to the point where Fergus arranges a marriage just to stop a scandal."

"You may find yourself agreeing to Fergus's marital dealings for other reasons," Marie warned her with a sly look.

"Who, Colleen?" Chloe snorted. "Never."

"You ladies look as though you've been rode hard and put up wet," Mr. Coney said once all four barrels had been taken from their bicycles into the pub. "I know it ain't proper for the likes of you to patronize my pub, but if you'd care to come inside and sit a while, I'll have Maeve make you some tea."

"A sampling of some of your weaker ale would be good enough for us," Shannon said, looking more like a fishwife than the eldest sister of an earl as she wiped her hands on her skirt and followed Mr. Coney into the pub. "We need to talk about the price of this shipment anyhow."

Colleen was more than happy to leave the business dealings of their brewing enterprise to Shannon. Shannon was the one with the head for business anyhow. Colleen fancied herself the sister with the finest palate and routinely adjusted the recipe for their beer. She had no qualms at all—even though she knew she should—striding into the backroom of the pub and following Mr. Coney's handsome young assistant as he directed her to a table near the door that led into the main part of the pub. She accepted a half-pint of ale and settled in to enjoy it, Marie and Chloe sitting at the small table beside her.

That was when she heard two familiar voices speaking low on the other side of the doorway.

"I need you to keep the dragon for me, Benedict." The man speaking had to be their cousin, Cailean O'Shea, Viscount Dervock. Colleen would know his melodious voice anywhere.

"Of course, I'll keep it." The reply came from Lord Benedict Boleran. Just the idea that Lord Boleran was in the next room, probably looking all smug and handsome —no, that wasn't the word she wanted to describe him— smug and *haughty*, had Colleen's temperature rising higher than it already was. She could feel her cheeks burning.

"Lord Boleran," Chloe whispered, then clapped a hand over her mouth and dissolved into giggles.

"Oh, dear." Marie rolled her eyes, her mouth tugging into a lopsided smile. She shook her head at Colleen.

"What are those reactions for?" Colleen hissed. "You know I simply cannot abide Lord Boleran."

"Oh, yes. You simply *cannot abide* him," Marie mocked her.

Colleen made a sound of disgust, even as she pressed a hand to her stomach. The ale she'd been served was stronger than she'd thought it would be, that must be it. Because there was no one in Ireland or beyond whom she hated more than Lord Boleran. Every time she'd encountered him, the man was stiff, morose, insufferable, and gorgeous.

No, that wasn't the word she was searching for either. Lord Boleran condescended to her in the worst possible way. He'd barely tolerated her visit several weeks ago, after Lord Kilrea's father and brother were killed in that unfortunate carriage accident, when Marie had implored her to ask Lord Boleran what he had observed about the wrecked carriage. He seemed to disapprove of her every time their paths crossed in town or at a ball. And yet, he always made it a point to torture her with an invitation to dance or a passing hello when she did not wish to speak to him.

Colleen's sisters continued to stare at her as if they knew something she didn't. She shook her head and deliberately ignored them, leaning toward the doorway to listen in on Lord Boleran and Cousin Cailean's conversation.

"...too big to put anywhere else," Cailean was saying. "And the poor thing requires such careful care and feeding, if you'll pardon the expression."

"Perfectly apt," Lord Boleran said.

"And what with my recent land sale...." Cailean let out a sigh. Colleen didn't need to hear him explain. They all knew that Cailean was strapped for cash and that he had resorted to selling off parts of his estate to pay his debtors. "The dragon will be better off in your care, for the time being," Cailean went on. "I trust you to keep it safe."

"The dragon?" Chloe whispered.

Colleen shrugged. She'd never heard of such a thing. At least, not outside of the world of fantasy.

"Your dragon will be welcome on my land," Lord Boleran said. "Provided it doesn't breathe fire and burn my barn down."

The two men laughed. Colleen was more confused than ever. Cailean was known to be eccentric, but if Lord Boleran was intent on indulging his fantasies...well, that was simply cruel.

"If you will excuse me for a moment," Cailean said. Colleen heard the sound of him getting up and moving away from the table.

Silence followed, which suggested Lord Boleran was seated at the table alone.

"I'm going to get to the bottom of this," Colleen whispered to her sisters.

Before any of them could stop her, she got up,

brushed her hair back from her face, squared her shoulders, and marched through the canvas curtain separating the back of the pub from the front.

The pub was only middling crowded, which relieved Colleen. Most of its patrons were seated at the front, near the windows. The back corner, where Lord Boleran sat alone at his table, was shadowy. It was the kind of place where nefarious men gathered to concoct dark deals. If it had something to do with a dragon, then whatever deal Cousin Cailean and Lord Boleran were discussing must have been dark indeed.

"How dare you?" Colleen asked Lord Boleran without so much as an introduction.

Lord Boleran was halfway through swallowing a mouthful of beer when Colleen accosted him. The pure shock of her arrival caused him to spit beer back into his mug and to descend into a fit of coughing. "Lady Colleen," he said, his eyes going round. "Whatever are you—"

"How could you play into dear Cailean's delusions by saying you'll house a dragon for him?" Colleen stepped closer to the table, working herself into righteous indignation. "Everyone knows Cailean is soft in the head."

"He is no such thing," Lord Boleran contradicted her. For a split second, Colleen thought she saw amusement in his cold, steel-blue eyes. Too soon, his expression hardened into offense. "Your cousin is a genius of the highest order. But more importantly, what in God's name are you doing in the back of a pub?"

"That is none of your business." Colleen tilted her chin up, but a quiver of anxiety shot through her gut. It truly wasn't appropriate for her to be there at all. She needed to get to the bottom of what Lord Boleran was up to by indulging Cousin Cailean, scold him as he deserved to be scolded, then leave. "What is this dragon Cailean seems to believe in?"

"My lady, this matter is none of your concern," Lord Boleran said with just the sort of imperiousness that irritated Colleen beyond all sense.

"You cannot take advantage of my cousin." Colleen snapped her back straight. "I will not allow it. And I demand you tell me what this dragon is."

"I have been sworn to secrecy, my lady." Lord Boleran fell into perfect, genteel formality. Colleen couldn't believe his audacity.

"I will find out what the dragon is," she told him, leaning in almost to the point where their noses touched. "Mark my words. If you harm my family in any way, you shall pay the price."

"A grave threat indeed," Lord Boleran said.

Colleen felt heat pouring off of him. Heat and the most delicious scent. Damn Lord Boleran for always smelling like fresh soap and the sea every time she encountered him. Damn him for having eyes like a winter storm, eyes she could lose herself in. He was her enemy, and she would do best to remember that at all times.

"Colleen," Shannon hissed from the doorway to the back room. "Come away at once. Our business here is done."

The reality of the situation closed in on Colleen. She glanced around. More of the pub's patrons were paying attention to the way she accosted Lord Boleran now. She truly shouldn't be there. If she or any of her sisters were caught in such a place, it would threaten their brewing business. As much as she hated to back down where Lord Boleran was concerned, she had no choice.

"This is not over between us," she hissed, holding up a finger.

She met his eyes and held them in a look of fire. Angry fire, that was, not the passionate kind. He stared back at her, his gaze unblinking as she backed toward the doorway. She kept her finger up as well, only lowering it at the last moment, before darting through the door into the back room.

Once away from Lord Boleran, Colleen let out a heavy breath. She felt the same way she had when they'd arrived at the pub—out of breath and flushed. It was simply because Lord Boleran got her back up. The man was a menace. If she didn't see him ever again, it would be too soon.

At the same time, she was determined to find out what the dragon was. If Lord Boleran was a danger to her family in any way, she would put an end to him.

. . .

THE MOMENT LADY COLLEEN DISAPPEARED INTO the pub's backroom, Benedict let out a laugh and shook his head. Colleen O'Shea was far and away the most unusual woman he'd ever known. She had the beauty and the breeding to be one of the finest ladies of the county, and yet she behaved more like a termagant than a debutante. Her appearance in the pub was startling for several reasons. First was the surprise of it all. What was the sister of an earl doing in a pub? Second was her physical appearance. Her face had glowed, as if she'd been engaged in physical labor a short time before, and her blouse had shown signs of sweat. Her bright red hair had been plastered to her forehead, but much of it was also wild and tangled. She'd clearly been out and about without the proper hat, which was shocking on the one hand, but completely expected behavior for one of the notorious O'Shea sisters.

If he were honest with himself, Benedict didn't know how he felt about the woman. She amused him and she horrified him. Her antics made him smile and made him frown. She was a scandal waiting to happen, but he was eager to watch that scandal play out. And she was beautiful. There was no denying that.

She wasn't a thing like Emily had been. Emily had been all demureness and restraint. Emily had bowed to his will on everything. But perhaps that was why she hadn't had the strength to endure childbirth. A woman like Colleen, on the other hand....

He shook his head and took a long swig of beer,

banishing the thought. It wasn't his place to imagine childbirth for any woman, let alone Lady Colleen O'Shea. Though he wasn't cold-blooded enough not to imagine what it might be like to get the wild woman in a condition to face childbirth.

"You look as though you've seen a ghost," Cailean said as he returned to the table. "And rather liked it."

"Not a ghost. Just your cousin, Lady Colleen." Benedict sent his friend a haunted look.

Cailean laughed. "What in God's name was Colleen doing in The Hangman?"

"God only knows." Benedict set his beer down. "One would think that since Fergus O'Shea has returned to Ireland, his sisters would make far less of a spectacle of themselves."

"Ah. It's Fergus's own fault for giving them those bicycles," Cailean laughed. "Though, if you ask me, those gifts were calculated on his part."

"How do you mean?" Benedict asked.

Cailean shrugged. "Fergus wants to marry them all off. They're all self-proclaimed modern women with an aversion to marriage. So finding husbands the traditional way will never work. My theory is that by giving them the means to get into trouble, Fergus has actually provided each of them with enough rope to hang themselves." He reached for his beer, but before taking a drink, he added, "It worked for Marie, didn't it? She and Christian Darrow are blissfully happy. And already expecting the Kilrea heir, if the gossip I've heard is correct. Fergus planned his strategy and executed it well with her."

Benedict tilted his head to the side, considering. Cailean had a point. Lady Colleen's presence at the pub seemed proof positive that she was getting into enough trouble to land herself a husband by accident.

The thought bothered Benedict. He didn't like the notion of Lady Colleen being any man's wife. Or perhaps it was that he didn't like the idea of the wild woman being any *other* man's wife.

He dismissed the dangerous thought, focusing in on his reason for meeting Cailean in the shadowy tables at the back of the pub. "There was another matter you wished to discuss with me?" he prompted.

"Yes." Cailean grew sober. He leaned across the table to Benedict. "I find myself in a bit of a bind after the land sale."

"It went through smoothly, did it not?" Benedict asked.

"As smooth as a fine, clear day," Cailean reported with a smile. That smile dropped. "I now have more than enough money to continue my aeronautical adventures. Except for one problem. I was paid in cash."

Benedict's brow shot up. "Cash?"

"Buckets of it," Cailean went on. "It seems that the bank wouldn't issue Farnham a line of credit, so he was forced to raise the funds in alternative ways. Alternative ways that resulted in a good, old fashioned chest of bills and coins."

Benedict eyed his friend warily. "He collected that money by legal means, I trust."

"He did," Cailean confirmed. "The problem is that I now have a chest of money—like some common pirate—and I need a place to bury it until I'm able to hire a secure wagon to take it to the bank in Belfast."

"And how long will that take?"

Cailean shrugged. "I've wired the bank to ask them to send a secure wagon and an armed escort, but I've yet to hear back from them. I think I need to make the journey to Belfast so that I can request assistance in person. And since I'll be leaving my estate, I need to store the money somewhere."

"Don't you trust your servants to look after it for you?" Benedict asked.

"I do," Cailean began slowly, rubbing the back of his neck. "You've heard the stories that are beginning to circulate about that gang of thieves in the county."

"I have." Benedict's brow darkened. In fact, the Murphy gang had terrorized County Antrim's wealthy all summer long. They'd stolen mostly from prosperous farmers and minor lords, but Benedict wouldn't put it past them to attempt to steal from a viscount like Cailean, if they thought they could get away with it.

"Your estate is so much larger and more secure than mine," Cailean said. "And as a marquess, one would hope the thieves would be too intimidated to invade the house and pull off a heist."

"That all depends on the amount of money," Benedict said.

Cailean sent him a look that said the sum was huge. His expression turned appealing. "Will you do it? Are you willing to house my pirate's booty and my glider while I make the trip to Belfast?"

"Of course." Benedict smiled and saluted Cailean with his beer mug. "I'd do anything for a friend."

Part of him had wanted to say he'd do anything for the O'Shea family. Lady Colleen's lovely, defiant face came to mind as he drank his beer. He had the worrisome feeling that he hadn't had his last bizarre encounter with the woman.

CHAPTER 2

"Dragon. Dragon." Colleen paced the floor of the large bedroom she shared with Chloe, biting her lip and rolling over the odd confrontation she'd had with Lord Boleran that afternoon. "Dragon. What could he mean by a dragon?"

Chloe—who was tucked into bed, her hair coiled in rags, resting against pillows propped behind her—lowered the book she was reading. "A dragon is a large lizard, often fire-breathing, and most certainly mythical," she said.

Colleen pivoted in her pacing and sent her sister a flat look from the other side of the room. "Yes, I know that much," she said. "I've read the same fairy tales you have. But that is precisely the point."

"That you've read the same fairy tales?" Chloe asked with a hopeful look.

"No, silly. That dragons are mythical."

"Sometimes I'm not so certain of that." Chloe tilted her head to the side, falling into one of her far-off looks. "Astronomically speaking, Draco is a great dragon in the skies."

Colleen tried not to roll her eyes at her sister and her penchant for astrology as she resumed her pacing.

"The ancients drew and named all of the constellations in the night sky," Chloe went on. "And it stands to reason that they named them after things they saw in everyday life—crabs, lions, twins, bulls."

"I can think of something that involves a lot of bull that I'm hearing at the moment," Colleen muttered.

Chloe was undeterred. "Well, if constellations were drawn after things the ancients experienced, then it would stand to reason that dragons once existed. Or something like them. I've read one theory that the first dragon was merely a very large crocodile that was described incorrectly, and that error of description grew out of proportion over time."

Colleen paused to blink at her sister. Sometimes there actually was method to Chloe's madness. "You don't suppose Cousin Cailean has asked Lord Boleran to keep a crocodile in his barn, do you?"

"Probably not," Chloe admitted. "But 'dragon' could be code for some other thing."

"Yes, that seems most likely." Colleen resumed her pacing. "But what?"

What sort of secret could Lord Boleran be hiding? From what she knew of the beastly man, he wasn't the sort to hide anything as interesting as a crocodile. Lord Boleran was a boor. He glowered at everything and everyone. He stood aside at parties, talking mostly to the men present and rarely deigning to engage any of the women in conversation. He was an excellent dancer, but that only made his aloofness harder to swallow. He was so dour, in spite of being one of the most attractive men in the county.

No, he most certainly was not. Colleen was astounded with herself for daring to think as much. It was true that Lord Boleran was tall with broad shoulders and strong legs. He had midnight-dark hair and cold blue eyes as well, like a romantic hero from one of the novels Chloe was forever reading. His lips seemed formed for kissing and his cheekbones were high and noble. All the ladies of the county whispered about him, wondering if he would remarry after his wife had died in childbirth several years ago. But no, the high and mighty Lord Boleran was too good to choose another bride from among County Antrim's elite ladies.

Not that Colleen cared what the man thought of marriage or whom he might marry. It certainly wouldn't be her. She was bound and determined to avoid Fergus's marriage noose as long as possible. A man like Lord Boleran certainly wouldn't allow any wife of his half the freedoms she enjoyed now.

Like the freedom to overhear wicked conversations about dragons in pubs.

"Dragon," she repeated, tapping her chin. "Dragon

has to mean something. A dragon in Lord Boleran's barn."

Chloe snorted suddenly. "You don't suppose that means something *wicked*, do you?" She wore a teasingly lascivious look when Colleen turned to glare at her.

"Even if it did, why would he be having that sort of a conversation with Cousin Cailean?" she asked.

"I've heard some men prefer other men," Chloe said with a shrug.

"Not Cousin Cailean," Colleen said. "And not Lord Boleran." She was certain of that much from the way his eyes smoldered when he looked at her, the way his tongue darted out to touch his lips, the way his cheeks flushed ever so slightly.

She sighed, frustrated with herself. "This is intolerable," she said, marching to her wardrobe. "Get up, Chloe. We're going to go solve this mystery right now."

"What?" Chloe sat straighter, eyes round as she watched Colleen pull clean clothes from the wardrobe and begin to dress. "Right now? But Colleen, it's past ten."

"Which will only make us that much more likely to discover the truth without being caught," Colleen argued.

Chloe threw aside her bedcovers and rushed to the wardrobe. "But it's gloomy and cloudy out. I heard Mrs. Pierce say her bones tell her we're in for a storm tonight."

"All the more reason for us to get over to Boleran Hall to discover the truth as quickly as possible. The faster we get there, the faster we can return home.

"Oh." Chloe let the single syllable draw out as she held her hands to her mouth, worry painting her young face. "I...I suppose neither of us will be able to sleep until we uncover the mystery."

"We won't," Colleen insisted with a nod.

They dressed in plain clothes, and Colleen slipped on her sturdiest pair of boots. All of the sisters had quite a few serviceable outfits that were more suitable for tradeswomen than aristocrats. Fergus hadn't made them throw out the clothes they'd worn at the cottage. Colleen was glad for them now as she wrapped a shawl around her shoulders, tucked the ends into the waist of her skirt, and grabbed Chloe's hand to tip-toe through the house and out to the stable, where their bicycles were stored.

There might have been some truth to the prediction that it would storm later that night. As Colleen and Chloe rode their bicycles through the dark, squinting to make certain they stayed on the road, flashes of lightning appeared in the clouds far in the distance.

"I'm not convinced this is a good idea," Chloe called from behind Colleen as they pedaled on, her voice high and tight with anxiety.

"It's a perfect idea," Colleen called back to her. "This is a perfect night for dragon hunting."

By the time they reached Boleran Hall, Colleen's legs were tired and her lungs felt as though they might burst, but she was filled with determination. The storm had inched much closer. The flashes of lightning were accompanied by loud booms of thunder. Tiny drops of rain were already falling as they reached the gravel drive that wound through the various out-buildings on the property of Boleran Hall.

The barn was set at some distance from the more refined buildings of the estate—the stables, the carriage house, and the gigantic and lofty manor house—but still within sight of the main house. Colleen studied the windows of the manor house—several of which were lit as though the rooms behind them were occupied. She wondered which one of the rooms was Lord Boleran's bedroom and if he was already in bed. Or perhaps Lord Boleran was still downstairs in a study somewhere.

Either way, his whereabouts were none of her business. She wasn't there to pay a social call, and the likelihood of him even knowing she was on his property was—

"Who goes there?"

Colleen and Chloe gasped and Chloe squealed at the harsh growl that surprised them from a stand of bushes near the barn. They skidded to a stop, feet leaving their bicycle pedals and hitting the ground.

"What do you mean, who goes there?" Colleen snapped out of panic. "How dare you accost me in such a rude manner?"

Her heart dropped to her feet a moment later as three shadowy men in homespun clothes with ruddy faces stepped out into their path. They were a motley group, and Colleen instantly had a terrible feeling about them.

"What are two misses like you doing out on a night like this?" the tallest of them said.

"I could say the same about you?" It was pure madness. Darkness was all around them. They were far from anyone who might be able to help them. Neither she nor Chloe had anything even closely resembling a weapon on them. All Colleen had was pride and a mad sense that if she pretended she were in charge of the situation, she might just be able to control it. "Be gone, you!" she shouted, tilting her chin up. "Or I will have the police arrest you for trespassing."

"Colleen," Chloe gasped. "What are you doing?"

"We got what we came for," another of the men muttered to the first, "and a storm's moving in. Best not risk it."

The tall man nodded, and without another word, the three intruders dashed off, disappearing into the night.

It took Colleen a few seconds of gulping and gripping the handlebars as the rain picked up around her before she felt as though she could move or speak. "We'd better move on too," she said in a wispy voice. "Before we encounter anyone else."

They rode on, taking their bicycles right up to the side of the barn. The rain seemed to go from a threatening patter to full pouring the moment they reached the side of the towering building. Colleen and Chloe were soaked within seconds. The downpour was so relentless that they were forced to leave their bicycles leaning against the outside of the barn as they dismounted and searched through the darkness for the door. Colleen cursed herself for not bringing a lantern.

"There has to be something in here to light things up," she told Chloe as they stumbled through the barn door.

They were out of the rain, but it was too late. Already, they were soaked to the bone. The barn smelled of hay and animal, and something else Colleen couldn't identify—almost like metal. She stumbled around, feeling her way, searching for a lantern or box of matches. Lightning and thunder continued outside, illuminating the darkness for split-second flashes that helped a bit, but mostly left her frustrated.

Suddenly, after one flash, Chloe screamed and grabbed hold of Colleen so tightly Colleen thought she might fall over. "The dragon!" Chloe squealed.

Colleen whipped around just as lightning flashed again. She nearly screamed as well as the huge shape of something with spreading wings was revealed for the space of a heartbeat. Colleen made a terrified, wordless sound, twisting back to the side of the barn and searching as quickly as she could for something to light the place.

Finally, her hands bumped into an old lantern and a box of matches. She thanked God for whoever had left it there as she fumbled for a match and lit it. A moment later, she had the lantern lit. Another moment after that, as light filled the vast space of the barn, she turned with Chloe and held the lantern up.

Both of them screamed again as the skeletal outline of a great, flying beast shone out of the darkness. It was just Colleen's luck that she fumbled the lantern in her fright.

She dropped it, and the moment the oil spilled across the straw near their feat, fire leapt up. They both screamed again, for an entirely different set of reasons, as flames spread in every direction.

BENEDICT LEANED BACK IN THE SUPPLE LEATHER chair at his desk, brushing his index finger across his lip as he read the letter he'd been sent by Ballymena's chief of police that afternoon.

"Your help in assisting our efforts to capture and thwart the Murphy gang are commendable, my lord. We welcome any contribution, financial or actual, that you choose to give. But we caution you against taking matters into your own hands. The Murphy gang is clever and merciless, and we fear for the wellbeing of anyone other than trained law-enforcement officials in any effort made to bring them to justice."

Benedict couldn't decide if he found the missive reassuring or insulting. He'd offered to help because, as a marquess, he had resources available to him that the police force might not have. Aside from that, a few of his more prosperous tenant farmers had been targets of the gang. He had a vested interest in catching the thieves and bringing them to justice. And now that Cailean's "pirate booty", as his friend had called it, was stored in an unused guestroom there in Boleran Hall, Benedict had the uneasy sense it was only a matter of time before the thieves appeared on his property.

It was his responsibility to care for the people who had been put in his charge through birth and heritage. He might not have shared all of the old mindsets of every member of his class, but he did feel as though his job in this world was to have a care for the lives and wellbeing of those who depended on him. He'd tried his whole life to live up to that expectation. He'd tried to be a good husband and a father on top of being a good steward of the land he'd inherited, but he'd failed miserably at that. Emily was dead, and so was their newborn son, and while that marriage had been one of convenience and class, not love, he wasn't so cold-hearted that he didn't mourn Emily's wretched fate. She'd been a good woman and a victim of her place in the world.

Lady Colleen O'Shea wouldn't sit idly by, sacrificing her life for a tradition that said her sole point in life was to produce an heir. Colleen would eke as much excitement and enjoyment from life as she could, Benedict was sure of it. He'd watched her gallivanting across the countryside with her sisters on their bicycles, seen her laughing and sampling far more delicacies than was proper for a lady at balls and banquets, and he'd observed her frolicking on the beach with children from the local school. Lady Colleen was full of life and...and why he was thinking of her when he should be focused on capturing a gang of thieves was a mystery. He should get up and see to the last of his business for the evening, or just go to bed. He should—

"My lord." His valet, Parsons, rushed into the room,

looking alarmed.

Benedict instantly sat up straight. "Is something wrong, Parsons?"

"There are intruders on the property, my lord," Parsons went on, gesturing for Benedict to follow him out to the hall. "Quigley is rousing the rest of the footmen to go after them, so I came to fetch you."

Benedict hurried after Parsons, pausing to grab a coat from the room near the front door before dashing out into the spitting rain. He knew better than to ask how Parsons and his first footman, Quigley, had stumbled across intruders in the dark on his vast property. It was better not to ask after the reasons the two young men might be out of the house on a night like that. What the two did on their own time was their business, as far as he was concerned.

Those thoughts were banished from his mind in a heartbeat as he and Parsons strode across the drive, searching the blackness for the most likely spot for thieves to be hiding. The rain picked up to an instant downpour, and Benedict turned up his collar, but that wasn't what arrested his attention. Far ahead of them, a tiny light in the barn flashed suddenly into a much brighter light. Its orange glow flared in the open doorway. It didn't take much to guess that a fire had broken out in the barn. The barn where Cailean's glider was stored.

"Hurry," Benedict barked, breaking into a run as Parsons followed.

A rush of excitement filled Benedict. They'd caught

the thieves at last. The blackguards had probably thought he would store Cailean's chest of money in the barn as a way to keep anyone like them away from the house itself. Or else they thought the glider was part of Cailean's treasure.

But as they grew close to the barn, the screams that echoed from it were not those of hardened, cut-throat robbers. The shrieks most decidedly were coming from women.

"A blanket! A cloak! Anything!"

Benedict nearly stumbled. He would recognize Lady Colleen's voice anywhere.

A second woman continued to scream instead of, Benedict suspected, being the least bit helpful. A moment later, a soaked figure with hair as red as the flames coming from the barn darted out into the rain and hurled herself around the side of the barn. Parsons broke off as if to catch her.

"Leave her," Benedict ordered. "We have to get the fire out."

He and Parsons dashed into the barn. Sure enough, Lady Colleen O'Shea stood, half surrounded by flames that she was trying to beat out with what looked like a flimsy shawl. A lantern sat on its side on the ground beside her, leaking oil that only made the flames worse.

"Get one of the horse blankets," Benedict shouted.

Parsons nodded and leapt to do as he was ordered while Benedict peeled off his coat. Acting fast, he leapt toward Lady Colleen, throwing his heavy coat on the lantern. Lady Colleen's eyes went wide, and she shouted wordlessly—possibly in outrage—as Benedict all but tackled the lantern. He wrapped it tightly in his coat, bundling the whole thing up and moving to hurl it out into the rain. Parsons raced to the fire with a horse blanket and began beating the flames.

Within a minute, the fire was out. Unfortunately, that meant that the barn was only illuminated by an occasional flash of lightning as the storm raged outside.

"Lady Colleen, what is the meaning of this?" Benedict boomed in the dark.

"I didn't—I dropped the—there's a dragon in your barn," she shouted at last.

"Yes." Benedict stepped toward her, rather enjoying the theatrics of the moment, now that his barn and Cailean's glider weren't in danger of being burned to a crisp. "And there's a trouble-making little minx too."

Colleen yelped, "How dare you?"

Benedict nearly laughed. Another burst of lightning and clap of thunder sounded from far too close by for his liking. They might have put the fire from the lantern out, but there was always a chance lightning could strike the barn. He was loath to see Lady Colleen hurt in any way, but the little troublemaker needed to be taught a lesson all the same.

"This is how I dare," he said, stepping into her and hoisting her over his shoulder.

Lady Colleen screamed in protest as he carried her out into the rain.

CHAPTER 3

"*L*et go of me, you brute! Put me down!"

Colleen thrashed and beat on Lord Boleran's back as he carried her, like a sack of potatoes, through the driving rain toward his house. Lightning continued to flash—one bolt landing throat-squeezingly tight to where they walked—and thunder boomed, but Colleen was determined to rage louder and fight harder than any storm.

"You cannot do this!" she hollered into the black and swirling night, even though Lord Boleran's shoulder wedged against her gut meant she couldn't draw in as deep a breath to scream as she might have otherwise. "You cannot manhandle me so. I am being kidnapped!" she shouted to anyone who could hear her. "I am being held against my will!"

There was no one around but Lord Boleran to hear her cries, though, and Colleen had the distinct feeling he was anything but impressed with her. As they neared the house, she sagged against his shoulder, settling for muttering invectives against him instead of struggling outright.

"You mangy cur," she growled. "You are no sort of a gentleman to treat me this way. You are the most vile, the most despicable, the most reprehensible—"

A sharp smack to her uplifted backside blew the words right out of her mouth, replacing them with a wordless cry of indignation.

"How dare you!" she gasped at the tail end of that cry.

"Lady Colleen," Lord Boleran's voice sounded above the rain and the vague sound of his boots crunching against the gravel. "Do shut up."

Colleen yelped. She inadvertently did as he said, simply because she was too outraged by his behavior to form another word. She flopped against him as he carried her up a slick set of terrace stairs and in through his manor house's front door—which was held open by a wizened and shocked butler.

"Mr. Conyers, please see to it that a room is prepared for Lady Colleen at once." Lord Boleran's voice seemed to echo through his vast front hall without the benefit of rain and thunder to drown out the sound.

At last, he put Colleen down, hefting her off his shoulder and lowering her to her feet, but continuing to grasp her until she had her balance. Only then did Colleen stop to consider how strong the man was. He had carried her as though she weighed nothing, and though she wasn't a hippopotamus, she wasn't as slight and willowy as Chloe or Marie. His shoulder had felt broad and strong under her, and she could feel how muscled his arms were through the soaked fabric of his jacket.

More than that, there was a certain, dangerous command in his eyes when she glanced resentfully up at him. He was infuriated with her, she could tell, but the flame in his blue eyes was as heated as the fire that had nearly consumed the barn. His dark hair was plastered to his forehead, but even the copious amount of water that dripped across his face couldn't dim the warm flush that painted his handsome face.

Good Lord, she thought as she blinked up at him. *Lord Boleran is like some devilish villain from a gothic novel.* And Colleen loved a good gothic novel. A stormy night, a handsome villain, being carried through the dark with nefarious intent. If Colleen didn't know any better, she would have thought she was about to be ravished.

Her pulse kicked up and her breath came in shallow pants that pressed her heavy breasts against sodden fabric of her blouse. "What do you plan to do with me now, Lord Boleran?" she asked, gazing defiantly up at him.

He gaped down at her, a certain degree of indignation joining the heat in his eyes. He moved slowly closer, leaning into her and bringing his face to within mere inches of hers. Colleen burned with—no, no, she wasn't going to name the feeling she burned with. She caught and held her breath, her gaze dropping to his lips.

"I am going to put you to bed without any supper," he said at last in a low growl that was...teasing?

Colleen's mouth dropped open. The blackguard thought she was a joke. He thought she was a child who had been disobedient and should be punished. Well, she was not a child, and she absolutely would not stand to be treated as one.

"You are a horrible, selfish man." She snapped away from him, crossing her arms. Her gesture of fortitude would have had more impact if she hadn't been dripping rainwater all over his entrance hall. In fact, she rather feared she looked like a standard-issue drowned rat. But that wasn't going to stop her from holding her own.

"Should I have left you to burn in the barn along with your cousin's flying machine?" Lord Boleran asked.

"His what?" Colleen pivoted back to him, suddenly curious.

He ignored her. "Or would you rather have drowned or been struck by lightning in the storm?"

"All of those options would have been preferable to being carted across your property like...like your property." Colleen turned her nose up. She hoped the gesture conveyed stubbornness and pride, but she feared it only made her look like the child he had implied she was. "You are cold and unfeeling and utterly incapable of any sort of tender human emotion."

"I am not—" Lord Boleran sighed and pinched the bridge of his nose, as though she were vexing him. She had yet to begin her attempts to truly vex him. That he was reacting in such a way to her now was a mortal offense. "You have no idea who I am or what feeling I am capable of."

"Oh, I know enough," Colleen insisted.

He merely stared at her, a combination of impatience and perhaps...hurt in his expression. "Come along," he said at last, stepping forward and cupping a hand under her elbow to escort her to the stairs. "While you were berating me for my inhospitality, Mrs. Ferrer headed upstairs, likely to prepare a guest room for you. Let's see if we can find you something warm and dry to wear until it's ready."

"I will not go anywhere alone in your house with you, my lord," Colleen protested, even as she stumbled forward, mounting the stairs when they reached them. "The scandal of an unmarried woman in your home at night, unchaperoned, is dire enough. I won't be manhandled into finding something warm and dry to wear as well. My reputation would never recover. And what has become of my sister? You cannot expect me to abandon her."

"Lady Colleen, you leave me at a complete loss," Lord Boleran said, raising his voice as they reached the top of his grand staircase and veered off to the left. "For I do not know whether to say 'I was unaware you had a reputation to protect in the first place' or 'Would you prefer to stand in the hall all night, soaking wet?' or even 'If you won't be convinced to wear something warm and dry, will you be wearing nothing at all?' Truly, the options for rebuttal that you give me are endless. And your sister has probably gone home, which means she has more sense than you."

Colleen yelped in offense, yanking her arm away from the odious man. "You, sir, are no gentleman," she said.

"And you, my lady, like that about me."

Colleen stopped dead halfway down a dim hall, lit only by a single lantern on a table farther down. A door was open past that, revealing light from a room. Colleen assumed it was the guest room that Mrs. Ferrer was preparing for her. But those assumptions were nothing to the outrage she felt at his statement.

"I like nothing at all about you, Lord Boleran," she said.

"Really?" He crossed his arms and leaned against the wall. The stupid man would probably leave a wet stain on the rather pretty wallpaper. "The way that you were looking at me downstairs told another story, my lady."

"I was not looking at you as anything other than a vile brute," Colleen argued, crossing her own arms to match him.

"You were undressing me with your eyes," he said, his wicked grin accusing.

Colleen sucked in a sudden breath as she realized he was doing the same sort of looking at her. More than that, the way her clothes were plastered to her body, he didn't have to have much of an imagination to envision what she might look like without her clothes. She should have dressed in more than a simple, linen shirt and plain skirt. She certainly hadn't donned enough undergarments to hide her shape when wet.

"Are we adding scoundrel to your list of faults?" she snapped, pulling at the wet fabric of her skirt so it didn't accentuate her legs and hips as much.

"Only if we're adding wanton to the list of yours," he said casually, still eyeing her.

"I am not a wanton," Colleen hissed. "I never could and never will think of you that way. You are nothing but an arrogant, stilted, boorish—"

He surged toward her before she knew what was happening. His large, warm hands cupped her face, drawing her closer to him. He slanted his mouth over hers, feasting on her lips as though they were delicacies. Colleen was so startled by his sudden kiss that she gasped, parting her lips. He took advantage of her shock, nibbling her lower lip before his tongue ventured into her mouth to brush against her own. He teased and tested her at first before deepening the kiss and invading her with full force.

At first, Colleen was too overwhelmed to react— either to protest or to join him. Her body softened against his. She leaned into him, lifting her arms to grip his sides, holding on for dear life. His tongue felt magical in her mouth, so she explored the sensation, kissing him the way he kissed her. He growled at her show of aggression, moving one arm to slide around her. With his hand splayed across her back, he jerked her closer, until their damp bodies met.

The sound of a woman clearing her throat farther down the hall broke them apart. Colleen stood where she was, stunned, her mouth open, for a moment before realizing Lord Boleran's housekeeper had stepped out of the lit room. Her eyes were averted now, and a flush covered her cheeks.

"My lord, Lady Colleen's room is ready," she said, her tone embarrassed. "I have taken the liberty of providing her with a robe and a nightgown as well. I'm afraid it is only my own nightgown, but it should do."

"Thank you, Mrs. Ferrer," Lord Boleran said. The man had the audacity to look sheepish over being caught in the sort of scandalous act he'd inflicted on Colleen. He gestured for Colleen to precede him down the hall to the room. "Could you have a maid run to Dunegard Castle as soon as the storm lets up to fetch suitable clothing for Lady Colleen to change into on the morrow?"

"Yes, my lord." Mrs. Ferrer curtsied, then hurried off down the hall.

Lord Boleran gestured again for Colleen to make her way to the room. Somehow, Colleen managed to gather enough sense to walk in the direction he pointed.

Once she had stepped over the threshold into a nicely-appointed, cozy room with a blazing fire that hadn't quite taken the empty feeling out of the room yet, Lord Boleran said, "I want no more trouble from you tonight, my lady. Do you understand?"

Colleen snapped straight. "You are the one who has taken liberty after liberty with me, my lord. Perhaps it is you who should be asked if they understand."

"I—"

Whether he was about to apologize or make some further excuse, Colleen didn't find out. She slammed the guest room door in his face.

A moment after the action was done and the resounding smack of the door quieted, Colleen slumped. That hadn't exactly gone the way she'd hoped it would. Granted, she wasn't entirely certain how she hoped it would go. Lord Boleran's kiss had been—

No, it was best not to think about that. Not to think about it at all. Though she touched her tingling lips as she walked deeper into the room, to where a robe and simple nightgown were laid out on the high, soft bed. She'd never been kissed like that before. She'd never had a man consume her so completely and make her feel so...so alive. Parts of her were still vibrating with excitement that she generally only considered when she was in the privacy of her own room. And her heart continued to beat as fast as if she'd ridden her bicycle all the way to County Down and back.

It was most certainly best not to think about any of it, but as she changed into the nightgown and robe, then brushed her hair out in front of the fire with the hair-brush Mrs. Ferrer had provided, her mind swirled with questions. Some of them had to do with Lord Boleran and his ungentlemanly behavior. Others had to do with the contraption she'd seen in the barn, not to mention the hollow and lonely state of his house. The majority of them had to do with Lord Boleran himself, though. Was he keeping her hostage for trespassing on his property? Would he truly send for a change of clothes for her, and did he intend to let her go home on the morrow? And did he have anything she might nibble on as a midnight snack? She was frightfully hungry from all the excitement of the evening.

Less than an hour after being shown to her room, Colleen tip-toed back out into the hallway in search of answers. There was nothing wrong with a little natural curiosity, she told herself, peeking into the darkened room next to hers. Curiosity was what caused mankind—and womankind—to advance.

There was nothing in the room beside hers. It was another guest chamber, not unlike hers. She crept on down the hall, looking into another unoccupied bedroom. Boleran Hall was huge, and it dawned on Colleen that she could search all night and not find what she was looking for. Especially since she didn't know what she was looking for.

She crossed the staircase and made her way down a second hall. One of the bedrooms there was feminine, but appeared to have recently had half of its decorations removed. Colleen wondered if that room had belonged to Lady Aoife, Lord Boleran's sister, who had recently been married.

She was debating the likelihood of that when she

stumbled across the oddest room she had yet to find in the house. It was not a bedroom. It might have been at one point, but most of the furniture had been removed. A few items were stacked in corners and covered with muslin. In the center of the room stood a table, and on that table was a chest. Curiosity burning, Colleen crept forward. She set the lantern she'd taken from her guest room on the table, then, biting her lip, she opened the chest.

She gasped at the sight of a great deal of money, both bills and coins, that the chest contained.

"What in heaven's name..." she started, but let the words fade.

She shifted a few of the stacks of bills and bags of coins to make certain that was all the chest contained. There must have been thousands of pounds of cash in the chest—far more than even a marquess, like Lord Boleran, would have on hand.

A thump somewhere in the house nearly scared Colleen out of her wits. She quickly closed the lid of the chest, grabbed her lantern, and hurried out of the room, shutting the door a little too forcefully behind her. Someone must have heard her walking the halls. She had to hide before she was discovered and...and who knew what.

To add to her fright, light was coming from under the door of the room next to the chest room. The hall wasn't unoccupied—like the guest hall, where she'd been tucked away. Sense told her to turn around and run back to her room, climb into bed, and sleep until morning. Colleen's sense of adventure told her to run forward and to find another room to hide in. Perhaps whoever was in the occupied room—she would be foolish to assume it was anyone other than Lord Boleran—hadn't heard her. Perhaps he would go back to sleep and let her continue to explore his house. Perhaps he would hear her and come looking for her, and they could repeat the kiss they shared in the—

Heavens, no! That wasn't her reason for creeping through the hallways in the middle of the night. She certainly wasn't that sort of woman.

But she was the sort of woman who pressed on instead of retreating. She scurried past Lord Boleran's door, diving for the closest door across the hallways from his and ducking inside whatever room that was.

As soon as the door clicked behind her, she turned to observe her surroundings. A faint hint of flowers filled the room, but it was cold, as though it hadn't been occupied for quite some time. But as soon as Colleen turned around, she was met with the site of a decidedly feminine bedchamber. The wallpaper was done up in shades of pink, the accessories on the vanity were most certainly that of a woman, and the bedclothes were frilly and light. Again, she wondered if perhaps this had been Lady Aoife's room, but one significant detail disabused Colleen of that notion right away.

A bassinet was placed right next to the feminine bed. Colleen's heart suddenly caught in her throat as she stepped quietly toward the dear thing. She swallowed hard, compassion and tenderness filling her, and glanced into the bassinet. A wild part of her wondered if she might see a baby, but reason and reality told her there would be none. More than that, there had never been one. The bassinet was, indeed, empty, and Colleen remembered a moment too late that Lord Boleran's wife and child had both died in childbirth.

Sentimentality and compassion overwhelmed Colleen as she reached out, fingering the delicate lace that decorated the edge of the bassinet. Women and babies died in childbirth all the time, but it was still the most horrible tragedy she could think of. It was, perhaps, the cruelest part of being born a woman—that so much pain could come in a moment that should have been filled with nothing but joy. She was never going to allow such a thing to happen to her. She would—

"What are you doing in here?" Lord Boleran's voice boomed behind her, nearly frightening Colleen out of her wits.

CHAPTER 4

*B*enedict scrubbed a hand through his hair as he stood by the fire, wearing nothing but the trousers of his pajamas, still slightly chilled from dashing out in the storm. Exhaustion pressed down on him, but instead of letting him climb in bed to sleep, an underlying restlessness filled his body. He hadn't planned on having such an eventful night.

Parsons had returned to the house shortly after he'd left Lady Colleen in her room and told him the fire in the barn was contained and that minimal damage had been done. That was a relief. But Parsons had also reported that Quigley had spotted at least three unknown, shadowy men leaving the property as the storm rolled in. They had to be members of the Murphy gang. Benedict was unsurprised that word of Cailean's money being stored at Boleran Hall had reached the gang. The men his footman had seen were likely the scouts, sent to figure out where the cash was hidden. There was no telling how much of the property they had scoured or how close to the house they had gotten before the storm had dampened their pursuits—literally and figuratively. It was only a matter of time before they would come back.

Quigley had had one other, amusing bit of information to report as well. Lady Chloe O'Shea was spotted fleeing from the estate. Apparently, the youngest O'Shea sister had been picked up by a carriage bearing Lady Coyle's crest, where Boleran Hall's front drive met the road. On the one hand, Benedict was glad Colleen's sister had made it home in the storm without suffering further danger. On the other, Lady Coyle was now involved. He might as well start having the marriage bans for his inevitable union with Lady Colleen read that Sunday because of it. Once she knew what had transpired that evening, Lady Coyle would insist on a wedding.

He sighed, giving his hair one last scrub and hoping it wouldn't dry at odd angles in the night, then headed for his bed. He supposed there were worse things than marrying Colleen O'Shea. She was lively and would keep him on his toes, that much was certain. His body had had no complaints at all to how she felt plied against him in the hall as he'd kissed her. He had no idea what had made him do it. In the heat of the moment, he'd assumed that the only way to make the chit quiet was to kiss her speechless. It had worked too...for about two minutes.

In truth, he was the one who had been stunned into

silence. Colleen had fire in her that went beyond her flaming red hair and her attempt to burn down his barn. Kissing her had inflamed him in ways he'd long since given up feeling. Not that he hadn't enjoyed a night or two with a willing woman since Emily's death. Carnal relief was not the same thing as enflamed passions, though. Colleen had responded vibrantly to their kiss, no matter what she might be tempted to argue about it. Benedict knew enough to know she would be just as responsive in bed.

After what Quigley had told him about Lady Coyle, he should have just taken Colleen to bed with him instead of depositing her in a guestroom at the other side of the house. It certainly would have been irregular and scandalous of him, but they both would have warmed up much faster and enjoyed the night much more than he figured either of them was enjoying it at the moment.

No sooner had that thought crossed his mind, as he was peeling back his bedclothes and contemplating the moral implication of stroking himself off while imagining what he and his houseguest could have been doing instead, a thump sounded from the room next to his. Benedict froze, listening carefully. He'd put Cailean's money in the unused dressing room beside his specifically so that he could hear if anyone dared to disturb the chest of cash. He doubted any of his servants would risk their position in his household by interfering with it. It was the rumored audacity of the Murphy gang that had convinced him to take such measures.

A moment after the thump, he heard footsteps scurry out into the hall and the door to the abandoned dressing room snap shut. Benedict let his shoulders drop and rolled his eyes at the sound of the floorboards in the hall outside his room creaking and the faintest, high-pitched gasp as a woman dashed past his room. None of the maids had any reason to be about the house at that hour and Mrs. Ferrer's voice wasn't that high. The interloper could only be Lady Colleen.

Shaking his head and rolling his eyes again, Benedict went to his wardrobe and fetched a robe. He threw it on, tied it in front, and marched out to the hall, jaw clenched. Colleen was going to be the death of him, he was certain. Although, judging from his body's reaction to the mere thought of her, it was going to be a pleasant death.

He shouldn't have been surprised that she'd scurried her way down the hall to Emily's room, or that she'd left the door open when he entered the unused bedchamber. Benedict hadn't bothered to enter the room for more than a year himself. He was surprised that the maids had kept it in such pristine condition, or that they hadn't removed the bassinet. An unexpected pang filled his heart—not out of any undying love he'd had for Emily, but because she'd been a good and loyal friend, and she hadn't deserved to die the way she had. That didn't stop him from frowning when he spotted Colleen brushing a hand over the bassinet.

"What are you doing in here?" he demanded.

Colleen gasped and spun to face him. He'd startled

her to the point where she nearly dropped her lantern. Frown deepening, Benedict lunged forward, snatching the lantern out of her hands.

"You nearly burned down my barn earlier," he said. "I'll not have you burning down the entire house in the same manner."

"I didn't...I wasn't...." She swallowed hard, the motion directing his gaze to the long line of her alabaster throat, then said, "There's no need to treat me like a child. You are the one who startled me."

Benedict let out a breath and shook his head. And here he'd hoped they could put their nonsensical argument to bed for the night.

"Lady Colleen, what are you doing in my wife's bedchamber?" he asked. He was certain he would get some kind of wild and vexing answer.

"Is this your wife's bedchamber?" Colleen asked with feigned surprise. Her cheeks flushed a fetching shade of scarlet as she glanced around. "I...I left my room in search of a bite to eat and I found my way here instead."

"In what way does this room resemble the kitchen?" Benedict asked.

"No, I don't mean that." Colleen frowned and sent him a look designed to wither him. It was just his luck that her defiance did exactly the opposite. He was grateful to be wearing a robe. "I meant that I...that I found my way to this room instead of back to my own bedroom after going in search...." She let her shoulders drop with a sigh. "Even I can't pull off an excuse like that."

"No, you cannot." Benedict set the lantern on Emily's bedside table so that he could cross his arms and glower at her. A tense silence fell between them. He rather liked the feeling of staring at her and watching her scramble for her next wild story to explain things. "I'm waiting, Lady Colleen," he said at last.

Colleen's uncertainty turned to a frustrated sigh. "I do not owe you an explanation for my nocturnal activities." She tilted up her chin, giving him another view of her neck.

Benedict found himself contemplating how delightful it would be to nibble on that perfect neck and to mark it as his. His robe wasn't going to hide much if he kept on devouring the sight of her and imagining things the way he was. "I'm waiting."

"For what?" she asked, perhaps even serious.

"For your explanation of why you are creeping about my house in the middle of the night like a specter instead of sleeping peacefully," he said.

"Oh, that." She lowered her head, seemingly penitent for a moment. At least, until she thought of an explanation. "You are the one who should feel sheepish, Lord Boleran," she said.

Benedict tilted his head to the side and studied her. So she felt sheepish, did she? "For what reason?" he asked.

"You are keeping secrets." She took a step toward

him, finger extended as though she would poke his chest. If she did, she'd likely find more than she bargained for in the current state of his body. "Why do you have a chest full of money in your home?" she asked.

He'd promised to keep Cailean's money safe until it could be transferred to the bank, and as far as Benedict was concerned, that included keeping it safe from his nosey cousins.

"Why are you in the marchioness's bedroom wearing nothing but a robe and a flimsy nightgown?" he asked, turning the tables on her. "Unless it is because you wish to take on the position yourself." He stepped toward her, fighting to keep from bursting into a grin as he teased her. "I can think of quite a few positions you might assume in a bedroom."

His intent was to shock and vex her into losing her temper and marching back to her guestroom. His advance on her only achieved half of its goal.

"You, sir, are a bounder." He'd stepped close enough to her that when she closed the space between them, she was able to poke him in the chest, like she had apparently intended to do from the start. "You have no respect for a woman's honor or her person."

"I have utmost respect for women," he argued. "If you were to simply look around you, you would see that."

Colleen inched back a bit, scanning the room as though some kind of documentary evidence—a contract or a manifesto—detailing his attitude toward women, would appear on the mantelpiece or Emily's vanity.

When she didn't find what she apparently wanted, she frowned slightly and bit her lip.

"I'm very sorry for your loss," she said, taking the conversation in a direction he didn't anticipate.

The pang in Benedict's chest returned, dampening the arousal he'd been enjoying just moments before. "Emily was a good woman," he said, lowering his head. "It was not a love match, but we were friends. We were both looking forward to the baby but...it was not to be." He stepped away from Colleen, frowning over the speed with which the mood in the room had changed.

Colleen continued to chew her lip and to wring her hands awkwardly in front of her. "I had no intention of bringing up something so painful, I'm sorry."

"Death is always painful," Benedict said. He glanced over his shoulder at her, then crossed the room to retrieve her lantern. Once he had, he extended a hand to her. "Particularly when it comes for someone so young."

Colleen studied his hand uncertainly. For a moment, Benedict wasn't sure if she would take it. Finally, she did. She let him lead her into the hall. Once there, he dropped her hand and shut the door to Emily's room.

"I suppose, as a marquess, you will need to marry again," she said when they were alone in the dark, quiet hall.

He almost laughed at her ignorance. He supposed he should tell her about Lady Coyle retrieving her sister or what that was certain to mean for the two of them.

Instead, he grinned rakishly and asked, "Lady Colleen, is that a proposal of marriage?"

Her eyes snapped wide. "Certainly not," she said. "I have no intention of marrying whatsoever."

She marched ahead of him. Benedict followed her. Clearly, Colleen intended to continue on to her guestroom, but when they reached Benedict's bedroom door, he grasped her hand again and tugged her inside.

Colleen squealed in that delightful, irritated, excited way she had as he shut the bedroom door behind them. "My lord, this is highly inappropriate. This is beyond the pale. This is...." She paused, her mouth dropping open as she took in the sight of his bedroom.

Benedict moved to put her lamp on his dressing table. His own lamps were all still lit, as was the fire, giving his bedroom a warm and cheery glow. It was one of the larger bedrooms in the house. He'd decorated it in a simple, homely way, in shades of blue with comfortable furnishings and artwork depicting scenes from nature. He had a bookshelf in his room, which was unusual, but he did like to read before retiring for the night. Colleen's eyes went straight to that. The literary lust he saw there reignited the desire he'd had for her earlier.

"So this is what a man's bedroom looks like," she said in an almost matter-of-fact voice.

Benedict grinned as he stepped up behind her. Yes, there were certainly worse things than finding himself trapped into marriage with Colleen—which would almost definitely happen tomorrow. Might as well get a jump on things.

"Do you like it?" he asked in a voice designed for seduction.

He slid his hands onto her waist from behind and bent close to her neck, breathing in her scent. A shiver passed through her voluptuous body as he tugged her back against him. That was more than enough to prompt his cock to stand up and take notice even more than it already had.

Unsurprisingly, after three beautiful seconds of sighing and sagging against him, Colleen jerked straight and pulled away from him.

"How dare you attempt to seduce me, you rotter?" she demanded.

"You're not exactly putting up much of a fight," he reasoned with a lopsided smile, stalking closer to her.

"If it's a fight you want, it's a fight you'll get." She balled a fist and raised it to shake at him.

He knew it would do nothing to improve his standing in her eyes, but he laughed. "Forgive me if I am not quivering in my boots."

"You're not even wearing boots," Colleen growled.

That only made Benedict laugh more. "That is precisely my point," he said. "Why fight when we could do other, far more interesting things instead?"

He wasn't so much of a cad that he would force her into his bed, but then again, judging by the sparks in her eyes, he wouldn't have to. She would come to him. Which meant all he had to do was stand where he was.

"Yes, we could do far more interesting things," she said, a light coming to her eyes. "Like you telling me why you have such a large sum of cash in a chest like...like a pirate's treasure in the room next to this one?"

Benedict threw his head back and laughed at that. Pirate's treasure was precisely how Cailean had described his money. Benedict supposed the O'Shea penchant for imaginative metaphors extended through the entire family.

"I have been sworn to secrecy," he said. It wasn't entirely true, but it made a better story than admitting he wanted to keep the presence of the cash quiet in case of thieves. "I have taken a solemn oath not to breathe a word about the treasure, just as I swore not to speak of the dragon."

Colleen's ferocity vanished for a moment. "Yes, what is that dragon anyhow?" she asked, her brow creasing in thought. "It looked rather like a mechanical prop for a theatrical exhibition."

"It's a glider," Benedict explained. Cailean was well known for being interested in flight—which was why a few, misguided souls, like Colleen, thought he was soft in the head—so he likely wouldn't care if his cousin knew what he'd been working on. "Your cousin refers to it as his dragon because of the shape of the wings."

Colleen cocked her head and blinked in thought. "Yes, now that you mention it, I do recall Cailean talking to Fergus about the Aeronautical Society of Great Britain." She paused for a few more moments before glaring at him once more. "You are attempting to distract me from my question with dragons and...and...." She waved a hand vaguely at his form.

Benedict glanced down at himself, amused to find that the front of his robe had sagged open, revealing more of his chest than was strictly proper for a young lady to observe. He couldn't have asked for a better way to aggravate her if he'd planned it.

"Are you distracted?" he asked, tugging at the tie holding his robe closed. He arched an eyebrow. "Are you curious?"

"No," she answered far too immediately.

"Are you certain?" he tugged the tie loose, letting the two sides of his robe fall open to reveal everything. And there was much to reveal. Not just his chest and stomach, but the significant bulge in his pajamas that he had as little control over at the moment as he had over Colleen on any given day.

"I'm—" Perhaps Colleen had intended to say she was certain, but her words turned into a squeak of interest.

The entire situation was certifiably mad, but Benedict hadn't had so much fun in...he didn't know how long.

"It could be argued, Lady Colleen," he said, holding his arms to the side so that his robe parted farther, eyeing her with heat and promise, "that you have compromised me in my own bedchamber."

"I did no such thing." Her voice was wispy with

desire, and she stared at his pajamas instead of looking him in the eye.

"You are the one who ventured out of your guestroom in the middle of the night," he reminded her, "venturing from one wing of the house to the other, and opening every door until you found me."

"That wasn't what I...." She closed her mouth, gulping. Her eyes snapped up to meet his. "Does that hurt?" she asked, inching closer. "You know, when it's...like that."

He shouldn't. Every fiber of his being told him he shouldn't. He had lifetimes more experience than Colleen. She was at a disadvantage in every way. And it would be unkind of him to laugh at her. But at the same time, the curiosity and the desire in her eyes were too much. He was only human, after all, and the way her breasts pressed against her thin nightdress and robe, the way her soft lips parted as she drew in short breaths, and the way she inched ever closer to him, peeking down at his erection, was far more than any man could be expected to endure.

And they would be engaged by the same time tomorrow night.

He absolutely couldn't resist saying, "You could come over here and kiss it better."

Her reaction was every bit as vehement as he expected it would be. She snapped her eyes up to meet his, anger radiating from her. "You are the very worst... the vilest...the most horrible...." She stomped right up to him, so close he could feel her heat and smell the salt of her skin. "I hope it does hurt," she hissed. "I hope this hurts too."

Benedict's soul very nearly left his body as she closed her hand over his cock. His eyes popped wide and he sucked in a breath so fast the edges of his vision went black. But whatever she'd intended to do, it certainly didn't hurt. She hadn't struck him or grabbed him tightly enough to cause pain. Exactly the opposite. Her hand was firm and caressing as she held him, only a thin layer of cotton separating them.

"Oh, my," she gasped. "That's...."

Blast the woman straight to hell, but instead of letting go, she stroked her hand up his length, eyes blazing with inquisitive fire as she measured him with her hand. Benedict steeled every nerve he had, forcing himself not to move as she studied him. As desperately as he wanted to wrap his arms around her and throw her on the bed so that he could have his way with her, he remained stock still. Lady Colleen O'Shea was about to have her way with him.

He let out a shaky breath, resting his forehead against hers as she reached down his length to close her hand around his balls. She sucked in a short breath, her sensual mouth curving into a wicked smile as she learned the shape of him. And, Lord help him, that wasn't enough for her. She drew her hand up again, then swiftly tugged at the drawstring cinching his pajamas at his waist. As soon as the knot popped undone, those pajamas sagged low on his hips.

She stole a quick, wanton glance at his eyes and bit her lip before reaching into his pajamas and stroking him free. The lip-biting might have been what sent him over the edge, or perhaps it was the way she gasped and giggled slightly at the sight of him. His tip was already slick with pre-come, which she felt the need to brush her fingertips over. Her touch on that over-sensitized part of his prick was like fire, and he growled at the glorious sensation.

That only seemed to spur her on. She slid her hand back down his shaft—which was iron-hard and throbbing as his heavy balls drew up. There was a chance he would regret it 'til his dying day, but Benedict closed his hand over hers, showing her how to encase him and stroke for the maximum amount of pleasure.

And, God have mercy, she was a fast learner. His breath came in sharp, shallow pants and sweat broke out down his back as she worked him, stroking faster and faster. He wasn't going to last a minute with her so intent on what she was doing. In all honestly, he didn't mind. He tilted his head back, vocalizing his approval and his pleasure. It was mad that a quick fumble—just her hand, not even her mouth—could bring him so close to completion so quickly, and he was certain it wasn't just because it'd been a while since he'd had a woman. It was her, Lady Colleen O'Shea, in all her wild, audacious, maddening beauty, stroking him off.

When the pleasure coalesced into white-hot light, gathering at the base of his spine and shooting through him like the lightning that he'd carried her through earlier, he let it happen. With a deep cry, he emptied himself into her hand, spilling across her delicate wrist. It felt so amazing that his bones threatened to turn to jelly.

Until Colleen let out a pure, ringing gasp of laughter. She leaned away from him, staring at his seed on her hand and wrist, and clapped her clean hand to her mouth, still laughing. Delight and arousal glittered in her bright, green eyes.

"I didn't know they did that," she laughed, nearly doubling over in amusement. "I didn't know."

Benedict didn't know if he wanted to laugh with her or frown and roll his eyes. All he knew was that his deflating cock was hanging out, and Colleen was staring right at it. "Colleen," he said, reaching for the sagging waist of his pajama trousers to pull them up. He took a half step toward her.

Colleen's laughter doubled, and she jumped away from him, lunging for her lantern, then leaping toward the door. "Goodnight, my lord," she laughed, throwing open the door and rushing into the hall.

Her joyful laughter echoed down the halls as she ran back to her guestroom.

Benedict closed his eyes, lowering his head and shoulders. For a moment, he shook his head. Then he, too, burst into laughter. That had to be the absolute most mad-capped thing he'd ever done. He continued to chuckle as he tied the drawstring of his pajamas, crossed the room to shut the door, doused all but one of his lamps, then dragged himself into bed.

He continued to laugh at himself and Colleen, rubbing a hand over his face and settling in to sleep. And judging by how relaxed and spent he felt after what he and Colleen had done, he would sleep well. At least he wouldn't have to bring himself off. He chuckled one last time before reaching to turn off the lamp by his bed. If tomorrow went the way he expected it to, he might never have to bring himself off again.

CHAPTER 5

*C*olleen didn't stop giggling until she reached her guestroom. Even then, as she washed the remnants of what Lord Boleran had done from her hand and wrist, she couldn't keep her giggles inside.

"Who would ever have thought?" she whispered to herself as she finished washing and skipped to her bed, discarding her robe, and leaping under the covers.

Who would have thought indeed? She'd caught a glimpse or two of a man's organ in the past, generally when she'd stumbled accidentally on a farmer relieving himself or once when she'd walked in on Fergus changing as a child. She'd never seen a man's...thing do what Lord Boleran's had done, though. It had been so big and so stiff and so...upright. And, of course, she wasn't entirely ignorant of the way of things. Marie had shared the secrets of being married with the rest of them shortly after her wedding to Lord Kilrea. But actually seeing a demonstration of the principles Marie had outlined in cryptic terms had been...breathtaking.

She snuggled against her pillows, closing her eyes and willing herself to sleep. It had been a long and exhausting evening, after all. But sleep stayed far away. Instead, she was beset by memories of Lord Boleran's body, of the strength and warmth of his broad chest and the dark hair that had covered it, of the glimpse of his thighs that she'd had, and yes, of his magnificent male instrument. It had been such a funny and intriguing shape, after all, and it had felt both soft and hard in her hand.

She wondered if he would let her touch it again. He'd obviously enjoyed her explorations. Though to be honest, at first she'd thought the sounds he made were those of discomfort. Upon reflection, she knew that wasn't true and that he'd taken great pleasure in her touch. His emission was enough to—

"Good Lord, Colleen, why are you dwelling on this so?" she scolded herself, flopping to her back and staring up at the canopy above her. "Stop it at once."

She did her best, but found that the only way to cease her thoughts of Lord Boleran's member was to become aware of how her own body felt in response. There was a distinct and delicious ache that seemed to pervade her more delicate areas. The more she thought about that, the more she wondered what it would be like if Lord Boleran returned her explorations in kind.

That did nothing for her ability to sleep. By the time morning rolled around and one of Lord Boleran's maids brought a fresh gown from home for her to change into, Colleen was anxious and sore after spending the night tossing and turning and barely drifting off. Which put her in the perfect mood to put up exactly the sort of resistance she should have to Lord Boleran when she met him downstairs for breakfast.

"Lady Colleen," he greeted her, already seated at the head of the table. He ate kippers on toast with one hand while reading the day's newspaper, which sat at the side of his plate. He wore reading glasses as well, which set Colleen's heart beating, for some odd reason. "I trust you slept well?" he asked, staring at his newspaper instead of looking at her.

After what they'd shared the night before, to be dismissed in such a way was unforgivable. Even if there were two footmen in attendance in the room who most likely should not see the two of them behaving in too familiar a manner toward each other.

"I slept terribly, thank you very much," she snapped.

She tilted her chin up and marched to the sideboard, where a variety of savory breakfast foods were laid out. It was not lost on her that, among those foods, was an entire plate of thick sausages. Their casings were curled back at the ends, giving the piece of meat an all-too distinct resemblance to Lord Boleran's instrument.

Colleen whipped around to glare at him. "Oh, you are beastly, aren't you?"

Lord Boleran glanced suddenly up from his newspaper, removing his glasses, his brow lifting in surprise. "I beg your pardon?"

Colleen jabbed a finger toward the plate of sausages. "You arranged these on purpose."

Lord Boleran's face colored, and he sent a furtive glance to one of his footmen. "I can assure you, I have no idea what you are talking about." The man had the audacity to look sheepish as he put his glasses back on and returned to his newspaper and kippers.

Colleen gaped at him for a moment, clenching her jaw as she attempted to decide whether he was toying with her or if he genuinely hadn't realized what his breakfast offerings resembled. In the end, hunger won out over anger—which it was want to do—and Colleen pivoted back to the sideboard. She helped herself to every offered delicacy before her, *except* for the phallic sausages. It would serve Lord Boleran right.

It did nothing by way of nurturing her irritation at Lord Boleran that the breakfast he served was delicious. Nor did it help that he asked her opinion of one of the items in the newspaper as regarded a recent gathering of adherents to the writings of Emeline Pankhurst. She still considered Lord Boleran a horrible cad for leading her astray the night before, for exposing himself to her the way he had as an irresistible temptation, for allowing her liberties and making the most alluring sounds as she'd touched him, for smelling of salt and skin and something wicked and desirable as—

Lord Boleran cleared his throat at the far end of the

table. The sound made Colleen realize she'd frozen with a fork full of eggs halfway to her mouth. The egg yolk dripped from her morsel like—well, never mind what it looked like. It was the wrong color anyhow. And she would not be held hostage by thoughts she could not control, thoughts *he* had put in her mind.

The brute.

The devil.

The way the sunlight streamed through the windows of the breakfast room, caressing his face and making his skin seem warm and alive and touchable was heavenly.

Colleen growled in frustration at herself and continued eating. She would make Lord Boleran pay for whatever spell he'd cast upon her.

"I suppose we should talk about what happened last night," the bounder said once they were secluded in his carriage, on their way to return her to Dunegard Castle. Her bicycle and Chloe's had been fastened to the back of the carriage, and she could see them through the rear window as she road in the backward-facing seat opposite Lord Boleran.

Colleen heated, and not just her face. Her entire body felt flushed with...with...with that nameless emotion that had kept her from sleeping all night. She opened her mouth, but hesitated before speaking. She had laughed in the moment, because the entire thing had been so amusing. She was angry this morning, because she hadn't slept well. But how did she truly feel about the situation? And should she continue to be amused by the functioning of the man's body, or should she disdain him for being so cold with her now?

"I don't think there's much to talk about," she said, opting for the path that would incriminate her the least. "You were a blackguard and I was curious. We both got what we wanted in the end."

She blinked as soon as she finished speaking. That wasn't what she thought she wanted to say.

The alluring, heated grin Lord Boleran sent her in return had her insides feeling like warm jelly. His blue eyes were surprisingly like flames. His lips were shapely and pulled slightly askew by his grin. All of which reminded her that she'd done more than just touch his person—she'd kissed him as well. And what a kiss it had been.

"That is not what I meant," he said, his rakish grin growing as he swept her with a look. "I meant that there will be consequences to you spending the night, unchaperoned, at Boleran Hall, whatever your reasons for snooping about my property. Which I still haven't had a proper explanation for, by the by. Regardless, I trust you know what the consequences of your actions are, and that you will be ready for the conversation that is surely about to happen."

"Oh, yes." Colleen crossed her arms, irritated to the point of sulking as she glanced out the window. They'd crossed onto Fergus's land and were now rolling up the drive to Dunegard Castle's front entrance. She knew precisely what would happen. Fergus would rail at her, then take her bicycle away and confine her to the house for God only knew how long.

"As long as you are prepared," Lord Boleran said. He didn't seem at all sympathetic to her plight.

The carriage stopped by the front door, and Colleen leapt down to the drive before Lord Boleran could hop down to offer her a hand. She squared her shoulders and marched ahead, intent on heading straight to her bedroom for a nap before facing her brother. She only barely noticed Lady Coyle's carriage parked farther down the drive.

"My lady, your brother wishes to see you and Lord Boleran in the drawing room immediately," Mr. Connelly, Dunegard's butler, greeted her.

Colleen let out an impatient breath and switched directions, heading to the parlor. It would be better to take her lumps up front and appear to accept her punishment gracefully so that she could be left in peace to nap.

She stopped short as soon as she entered the parlor. She'd expected to find Fergus lounging near the window, reading a book, or something along those lines, while Henrietta, her sister-in-law embroidered on the sofa near him. Or perhaps Henrietta would have her and Fergus's son down for playtime, and Shannon and Chloe would be cooing over the boy. She didn't expect Shannon and Chloe to be there at all, but they were. Shannon sat as demurely as it was possible for Shannon to sit on the sofa near Henrietta, while Chloe was slumped guiltily on one of the chairs across from the sofa. And of all things, Lady Coyle sat imperiously in the chair beside Chloe's looking as though someone had put nettles in her tea.

"Ah. At last," Lady Coyle said as Colleen took a tentative step into the room. "They have returned." There was so much weight and doom in her simple statement that Colleen found herself swallowing a lump in her throat.

She was all too aware that Lord Boleran had caught up to her and now stood behind her in the parlor's doorway. The man had the audacity to tap the small of her back to prod her into entering the room fully.

"Lord O'Shea," he said with a quick nod of his head. "I have come to return your sister."

"I would thank you, Lord Boleran," Fergus answered, a peculiar grin tugging his mouth to one side, "but I have a feeling you haven't returned her for long." He sent a glance with his one remaining eye to Lady Coyle. With his eye-patch and the wicked amusement painting his face, Fergus looked more like a pirate than ever.

"Understood, my lord." Lord Boleran matched Fergus's infuriating grin, bowing slightly. "And I expected as much."

"So you're willing to accept the consequences?" Fergus asked.

"I am, my lord." Lord Boleran squared his shoulders and leaned ever so slightly toward Colleen.

Colleen let out an impatient breath, throwing up her hands. "Will someone please translate this odious language of male-speak so that I know what is being discussed?"

Lady Coyle reacted as though Colleen had aimed a dart at her. "Surely, a woman of your breeding would know that she could not stay the night alone in a gentleman's house without reaping the consequences of those actions. We are not heathens, my dear."

"Yes, I know that I will be punished, Lady Coyle, and I know—" Colleen stopped, closing her mouth and frowning at the august woman. "I beg your pardon, my lady, but how do you know where I passed the night?"

"I didn't mean for anything to happen, Col, honestly." Chloe jumped suddenly from her chair. "I should have warned you about going out last night. Saturn is close to a conjunct with Jupiter at the moment, and Mercury is in retrograde, so mechanical things were bound to malfunction. It was an ill-advised trip from the start and—"

"Child, whatever are you going on about?" Lady Coyle glanced to Chloe as though she'd sprouted a tail. She clucked her tongue and glared at Colleen. "I was returning from an evening at Lord and Lady Toome's estate. They are entertaining Lady Toome's cousin, the Duke of Blackburn, so of course I was invited for supper."

"Of course, my lady," Lord Boleran said with a deferential nod. He was smiling and his eyes were shining, as though he were on the inside of some sort of joke. Colleen narrowed her eyes at him.

"On my way home, I discovered this unfortunate

child, bedraggled and shivering in the storm." She gestured to Chloe. "I rescued her and brought her home, of course, and on the way, she regaled me with a tale of Lord Boleran carrying Lady Colleen over his shoulder and up to his house."

"I should have gone back to save you," Chloe blurted. "Especially when I saw Lord Boleran carry you away from the barn. But I was frightened, and I feared those men would come after me, and Lady Coyle was there with her carriage. I begged her to return to Boleran Hall to rescue you, but she told me the damage had already been done."

Slowly but surely, the full reality of the situation Colleen found herself in began to sink in. Marie had found herself engaged earlier that summer for a far lesser sin than spending the night at a gentleman's home. While Colleen thought the whole thing was ridiculous, she suspected Lady Coyle would not share her views.

"Benedict." Fergus addressed Lord Boleran in a far too familiar way. "Are you prepared to marry my sister, to preserve her honor, and to prevent a scandal?"

"Good heavens, it's not as bad as all that," Colleen yelped before Lord Boleran could answer. "All I did was spend the night at his house."

Colleen could have strangled Lord Boleran on the spot for the guilty way he tilted his head to the side and winced slightly.

"Colleen?" Fergus asked, managing to convey ten

times the disapproval with just one eye that he might have conveyed if he'd had both.

"There doesn't need to be a scandal," she insisted, her pulse kicking up and a fine sweat breaking out down her back. "Not even the servants were aware that I ended up in his room when I went exploring after dark."

"Colleen." Fergus's voice turned dark, and he sat back in his wheelchair, crossing his arms.

"This is all just a part of your nefarious scheme to marry all of us off against our will." Colleen took a step toward him, pointing an accusing finger. "I will not be passed off on a man I detest simply because you do not wish to have free and progressive sisters."

"Colleen," Fergus repeated, slightly more exhausted.

"It is not as though my honor was ruined in any way," Colleen pressed on. "If anyone's honor was compromised, it was Lord Boleran's. He's the one who all but removed his clothes and let me touch his—" She stopped, gulping. Blast her and her impulse to prattle on until she talked herself out of trouble. She should have known by now that every attempt she made to dig herself out of a hole only buried her deeper. But the frustration of being told she should keep silent and let the menfolk run and ruin her life was too much of an insult to be born. "I will not marry Lord Boleran," she insisted, albeit weakly. She had a horrible feeling she was defeated.

"There is no need for a particular rush," Lord Boleran told Fergus, almost apologetically, his tone peculiar, frustrating Colleen even more. "Though I will understand if you wish to hasten proceedings."

"I am not marrying you," Colleen said, whipping to face him. "I do not even like you."

The teasing grin Lord Boleran gave her in return said that he knew that wasn't true.

"I believe a six-week engagement would suffice," Lady Coyle said. "It is not so much that time will be wasted, but not so little as to cause speculation and scandal."

"There is nothing to speculate about," Colleen insisted through a clenched jaw. "I have no wish to marry. Anyone. Not just this lout."

"Remind me to share a few tips for dealing with strong-minded women, Benedict," Fergus said, daring to chuckle as he spoke. "I believe you're going to need them."

"I believe you are right," Lord Boleran replied.

"You are horrible," Colleen said, glancing between Fergus and Lord Boleran. "Both of you. I refuse to fall into your trap the way Marie did."

"But my dear," Lady Coyle said with a combination of impatience and indignation, "you will be a marchioness."

"I would rather be a fishwife." Colleen balled her hands into fists.

"That could be arranged," Fergus said in a flat voice. Colleen opened her mouth to argue with him, but Fergus held up a hand to stop her. "Enough of this. I've indulged the lot of you too much by staying in England for so long, and I'm beginning to think I've gone too easy on you since returning as well."

Shannon and Chloe sat up and took notice at that statement. Their eyes went round, as if they saw the writing on the wall and knew that they were next.

"You will marry Lord Boleran," Fergus said with finality. "And you will count yourself grateful. Benedict is a good man and a good friend. I trust him with my sister." He narrowed his eye at Colleen. "I trust him, which is more than I can say about you, dear sister."

"This is intolerable." Colleen threw up her hands. "I've never been so insulted in my life. I will not stand for this."

She turned to head out of the room. As she did, she sent a scathing look at Lord Boleran. The man had the nerve to look apologetic. And handsome. She would never forgive him for looking so handsome as he watched her storm from the room, following her with those electric, blue eyes of his. She was furious with him for the way his gaze made her feel.

And she would stand by her word. She had no intention of marrying Lord Boleran, even if it meant she would be a marchioness. If it was the last thing she did, she would find a way to stop the wedding.

CHAPTER 6

"There has to be a way out of this travesty of justice," Colleen said the next afternoon, as she paced the length of Marie's newly redecorated parlor at Kilrea Manor. "I cannot believe Fergus would be so cruel as to force me to marry that lout, Lord Boleran."

Her sisters didn't respond immediately. At least, not with words. The three of them exchanged looks. Shannon reached for her teacup and took a long sip, avoiding Colleen's eyes. Marie fussed with a lace doily on the arm of the chair where she sat. Even Chloe seemed far more interested in the blank corner of the ceiling, where the walls met, as though the secrets of the universe were contained there.

"You do agree with me, do you not?" Colleen asked, brow pinched in frustration.

"We agree with you in principle," Shannon answered

after swallowing her tea. "It is entirely unfair of Fergus to force us into marriages that we do not want."

"Do not want being the operative words in this situation," Marie said in a quiet voice. A bit too quiet.

Colleen narrowed her eyes at her. "And just what, dear sister, do you mean by that?" She clipped her words, pacing closer to Marie and perching on the matching chair opposite her.

Marie studied her, biting her lip, for a long moment before letting out a breath. "Believe me, I never thought I would say this," she held up her hand, "but marriage is not the hellish punishment I once thought it would be."

Colleen scoffed. Chloe glanced away from her fascinating corner, eyes going wide.

Shannon scooted forward in her chair and cleared her throat. "Yes, dear, but part of the reason you feel that way is because you stumbled across your own groom, quite by accident."

"And he's ever so handsome," Chloe said with a broad grin. "And, what with you being a Scorpio and him a Pisces, it was bound to be a perfect match."

Marie and Shannon exchanged an amused look. Shannon covered her mouth, glancing fondly at Chloe, even though Chloe didn't see the look.

"The point is," Marie went on, "that marriage isn't the end of the world, as we once assumed it was. There are a few decided advantages to the married state." She blushed furiously, bursting into a giggle before she could stop herself. She reached for her teacup, but before she took a sip, she said, "Advantages that are particularly enjoyable after dark." She paused. "Although they most definitely aren't limited to nocturnal hours."

Colleen let out an impatient breath and stood to resume her pacing. "You are referring to sexual relations, of course," she said. "No need to pretend to be delicate about it. Not anymore."

"Good Lord, what is that supposed to mean?" Shannon asked, her back snapping straight. "Did more happen at Boleran Hall the other night than you have revealed?"

"No!" Colleen balked. A moment later, her shoulders sank and heat flooded her face. "That is to say, nothing as exciting and...comprehensive as all that." Once again, she'd opened her mouth and let more come out of it than she'd intended to. One day, she would learn to be as silent as the grave.

But at least she wasn't as bad as Chloe.

"Colleen told Lady Coyle that she'd touched Lord Boleran's willy," she informed Marie.

Marie nearly spit her tea. "You did not," she gasped after swallowing.

Colleen spread her arms to the side and let them drop in a helpless gesture of admission. "It was right there, plain as you please," she said. "Lord Boleran was the one who untied his robe so I could see the...the bulge in the first place. He lured me into it, I tell you. How was I supposed to resist temptation, especially when he didn't pull away or stop me when I loosened his pajamas?"

All of her sisters looked at her in disbelief.

"Why on earth was Lord Boleran in a robe and pajamas?" Marie asked.

"You haven't heard the entire story yet," Shannon answered with a warning look. "Apparently, the same curiosity that killed the cat led our dearest Colleen to leave her guestroom in the middle of the night so that she could creep into Lord Boleran's bedroom in order to fondle him."

"That is not what happened at all," Colleen growled, marching back to the circle of chairs and sofa where her sisters sat. "I did not intend to end up in his bedroom. I certainly did not intend to handle his private member to the point where it burst."

"It what?" Shannon gasped.

"Do you mean it exploded?" Chloe went pale.

Marie rolled with laughter, spilling tea as she did. She put her teacup down and hiccupped a few times as she tried to draw enough breath through her amusement to say, "If you found that enjoyable, just wait until you attempt to get the same results with your mouth."

Colleen, Shannon, and Chloe all snapped their attention to her with wide eyes.

"Oh, don't look so shocked," Marie went on. "It's absolutely delightful, provided one doesn't go too fast or attempt to take too much at once. And husbands are more than happy to return the favor with some tricks of their own."

"I can't even...why would you even mention such a...

this is absolutely preposterous." Colleen threw up her hands, sinking into her chair once more. "I am not going to repeat the experiment with Lord Boleran—with my hand or with my mouth." Though she did find herself wondering what that part of a man tasted like, and if it was anything like the feel of his tongue in her mouth when she'd kissed him. She shook her head to clear those disturbingly erotic thoughts away. "The point is that I do not want to marry Lord Boleran."

"Are you certain?" Shannon asked. She still looked a bit stunned from Marie's admission, but she seemed to gather her wits quickly. "You always have been...aroused by the man."

"I believe the word you are looking for is just 'roused' without the 'a'. As in, angered. As in, every time our paths have met, the man vexes me to distraction."

"Which is a sign of a deeper attachment," Shannon said.

"Especially with you being a fire sign," Chloe added.

Colleen sent her a withering look. "This is not helping. I wanted the four of us to meet today, away from Fergus's prying ears, to discuss ways to force our brother to call off the engagement."

Her sisters exchanged looks. "I don't think there's a single chance he will, dear," Shannon said.

"Especially after what you've told me," Marie added with an amused grin. "Besides, it sounds as though Lord Boleran is in favor of the match."

"Only because he knows it will give him the ability to

vex me every day for the rest of my life," Colleen said. "Which will be short, as I'm sure I will expire from irritation before the end of the year."

"No one has ever died of irritation...have they?" Chloe asked, blinking.

Colleen ignored her. "We need to discover something about Lord Boleran that is so wicked, so devious, so dire, that even Fergus will agree we should not be wed."

"I doubt such a thing exists," Marie said. "Christian is friends with the man, and he speaks very highly of him."

"Fergus has been friends with him for decades too," Shannon added.

"I know Lord Boleran must have something dark in his past that would prevent Fergus from allowing me to marry him." Colleen thought for a moment. An idea struck her, and she sat straighter. "The money," she said.

"What money?" Marie asked.

Colleen leaned closer. Her sisters followed suit, closing their circle. "When I was exploring his house, I stumbled across a room. It contained nothing but a large chest. And in that chest was money. Cash. Bills and coins."

"Lord Boleran is a marquess," Shannon argued. "And I've been told his estate is prosperous."

"But what sort of man keeps that large a sum of cash in his possession?" Colleen asked, her mind popping with more and more ideas as she remembered what she'd seen. "Every nobleman I know keeps their money in a bank. If they need to spend it, they either do so in small amounts or they write bank draughts to cover large purchases."

"That is true," Shannon said.

"So why does Lord Boleran have a chest of cash in the room next to his bedchamber?" Colleen asked.

They were all silent for a moment before Chloe gasped loudly, jerking upright. "What if he is in league with those robbers who are terrorizing the county?" she asked, placing a hand on her chest.

Shannon frowned. "The Murphy gang?" She made a scoffing noise. "They are petty hooligans."

"But even petty hooligans need a ringleader," Colleen said. She grabbed hold of the idea and ran with it. "I'm certain that's it. Lord Boleran is in league with the Murphy gang."

"It doesn't seem very likely," Marie said. "That Murphy gang has been robbing mostly wealthy farmers and tradesman. They operate nearer to towns. One of Christian's tenants was a victim of the gang just last week. As I said, he and Lord Boleran are friends, so why would one friend tell his gang to attack the tenant of another friend?"

"Because Lord Boleran is just that wicked." Colleen's blood coursed through her veins. She was certain she was right. Or, if not, that she wanted to be right. She wanted Lord Boleran to be a villain, and she was willing to endure great leaps of logic to make it so. "All I need to do is prove that Lord Boleran is in charge of the Murphy gang, show my proof to Fergus, and he will call off the engagement at once."

Her sisters were silent. At least, until Shannon reached a hand to pat Colleen's where it rested on the arm of her chair and said, "Dearest, I believe you have read too many gothic novels."

"You do enjoy the macabre a little overmuch," Chloe added. "I tried reading one of those books you like, and I couldn't sleep for a week."

"We all have vivid imaginations," Marie added.

"I am not imagining things," Colleen insisted. Though if she were honest with herself, a tiny voice in the back of her head said that she was being an utter fool. There was no possible way Lord Boleran was involved with common thieves. She was grasping at straws because she had foolishly fallen for Fergus's marriage trap. No, it wasn't even that. She'd trapped herself with her outlandish curiosity. Her pride was wounded.

But could she truly be blamed? The life of a lady was dull as toast in the best of times. She'd enjoyed living in the cottage with her sisters, fending for herself and making her own way through life. Now that she'd had a taste of how interesting life could be for a woman, it grated on her that she was being asked to revert to the stale, boring life that women were told to live. She wanted so much more than that. She wanted excitement and adventure. She wanted to feel as though she were worth more than to be a trinket on a man's arm or a means to provide him with an heir. Lord Boleran's first wife had done her best to fulfill that duty and it had killed her. Colleen wasn't ready to die—not physically, and not emotionally.

"I'm going to prove Lord Boleran is a thief and a bounder," she said, rising. "I'm going to prove it, and Fergus will have to let me out of this engagement."

She marched out of the room and out of the house, fetching her bicycle and heading home. Frustration followed her all the way. She knew she should be content with the marriage Fergus had arranged for her. She had to admit that the sparks she felt for Lord Boleran weren't entirely antagonistic. He was intelligent and challenging —perhaps a little too challenging. If boredom was her fear, there was an even chance she wouldn't be bored as the Marchioness of Boleran. But there was also a chance Lord Boleran would stifle her once he was her marquess, that he would treat her the same way every woman was treated.

Well, if he wanted to master her, if he wanted to be her marquess, he was going to have to prove not only that he wasn't hiding anything underhanded, but also that he could make her happy and let her be free.

The plan was simple. She bided her time through the afternoon, choosing the perfect outfit for unmasking thieves and blackguards, and waited until the rest of her family had gone to bed. Fortunately for her, Chloe was exhausted after her day and fell asleep fast, enabling Colleen to don her spying clothes and tip-toe out of her room.

She wasn't as lucky when she crept out of the house to the stable, where their bicycles were kept. Just as she was wheeling hers out into the open, she crossed paths with Shannon coming home.

"What are you doing?" Shannon asked in surprise.

"I could ask the same of you," Colleen told her.

Shannon made an impatient noise and dismounted her bicycle to wheel it into the stable. "I was at the cottage, checking on the latest batch of beer. And now it's your turn."

"I'm going to Boleran Hall to gather evidence against Lord Boleran," Colleen admitted.

Even in the dark, Colleen could see the censure in Shannon's eyes. "Don't be a fool, Col," she said. "It's late, and you've already gotten yourself into trouble by raiding Boleran Hall once. Besides, the Murphy gang is still on the loose. You've no idea what they would do if they encountered a helpless woman such as yourself."

"I am far from helpless." Colleen thrust her chin up. "And if you're so worried, what are you doing out at this hour? Why not stay at the cottage?"

"I am coming home," Shannon argued. "This is the end of my night and my return to safety. You are just going out. I might be a fool, but you are a bigger one."

"You won't say that when I prove that Lord Boleran isn't worthy to marry me," Colleen said, stepping on one of her bicycle's pedals. "I won't let you talk me out of this, Shannon. You'll see. By morning, I will have freed myself from the scourge of Lord Boleran, and

Fergus will never try to thrust me at another man again."

She stepped on the other pedal, moving forward into the night as Shannon called after her with, "Colleen, wait! Don't go out there."

Colleen ignored her, pedaling as fast as she could to get away from her doubting sister, her meddling brother, and her entire, miserable life. She was going to take her life into her own hands, no matter what. And if Lord Boleran caught her creeping about his home, then he could just do to her what he'd done to her the last time.

Colleen nearly rode straight off the road as the thought entered her mind. She was shocked with herself and had no idea where the notion came from. Surely, she didn't want Lord Boleran to catch her. That couldn't be the reason she was flying off to his house in the middle of the night. She prayed that she didn't run into him at all, that she could sneak inside and get the proof of his villainy that she needed without seeing the man at all. It wasn't as though she wanted to *see* him, any part of him. Or kiss him. She didn't want that either.

"Ugh, you ninny," she cursed herself, pedaling on through the night. It was Marie's fault for filling her head with notions she shouldn't be contemplating, notions of taste and texture.

The grounds of Boleran Hall were quiet as Colleen rode her bicycle up the gravel drive. She turned aside at the barn, wheeling her bicycle inside. The barn still smelled charred, but she knew the building and figured it would be the safest place for her bicycle. Once it was carefully stowed, she tucked the shawl she wore tighter around her shoulders and sped up to the house in the shadows as fast as she could.

She wasn't certain how she would get in. Grand houses were well-attended by staff, but they had so many windows and doors that something had to be unlocked and abandoned. She thought about trying to get in through the kitchen door, until she spotted a scullery maid scrubbing pots in the courtyard just outside of the door in question. The front door wasn't an option either. Her only choice was to creep around the house, testing windows and French doors.

The task felt as though it took forever, but at last she discovered that one of the French doors in the conservatory—where she'd once heard Lord Boleran and his sister perform for guests—Lord Boleran had a surprisingly clear tenor voice—which she should not have been thinking about at the moment—was unlocked. She pushed it open and held her breath as she crept inside, celebrating her victory with a tiny squeal of delight.

It had been easy to break into the house—perhaps a bit too easy, if she were honest—and it was simple to shuffle quietly from the conservatory and into the hall. The grand staircase was just outside of the conservatory, which was convenient. It meant she didn't have to go very far before creeping upstairs.

The hall she tip-toed down was exactly as it had been two nights before, but it felt entirely different. Colleen was all too aware that she was an interloper now and not a guest. She had no convenient guestroom to run to if she should encounter a servant. Which meant she had to be as quick about her mission as possible. She remembered exactly where the room with the chest was located and flew there as fast as she could without making the floorboards in the hall creak.

Once she was there, she celebrated with another silent squeal of victory and tried the door handle. As it had been the other night, the door was unlocked. She couldn't believe her luck. Surely, Lord Boleran would have left some sort of proof of his villainy along with the cash. She'd only had the briefest glimpse of the money the other night, but she'd been sure there were notes of some sort along with the bills and coins. Or so her imagination told her. They would contain all the evidence she needed of wrong-doing, all the proof Fergus would need to call off the engagement. She could taste freedom already. She could—

As she pushed open the door, it bumped something on the other side. Whatever it was, within a split-second it crashed over. The sound of hollow metal clattering to the ground—like a thousand bells ringing in cacophony—roared from the chest room. The racket was unmistakable, as was the sudden thump and scurry from the bedroom across the hall.

"Stop, thief!" The door on the opposite side of the hall, farther down, flew open as well, and two of Lord Boleran's male servants leapt out, cudgels in their hands.

Colleen screamed. One of the servants shouted in shock as well.

For a moment, the three of them gaped at each other in disbelief. Then one of the men—she believed it might have been Lord Boleran's valet—said, "I'll be a monkey's uncle. It's her again."

CHAPTER 7

*B*enedict had no idea how much work was involved in planning a sudden wedding. He sat at the desk in his study, poring over the list of instructions Lady Coyle had given him after they'd departed Dunegard Castle two days ago. After Colleen had run from the room in a temper over the fact that she had no choice but to marry him. He felt sorry for her. At least, to a degree. It was a simple fact of the way things were that women had fewer choices in whom they married and when than men did.

Not that he'd had any choice either, once Lady Coyle became involved.

Benedict frowned at the list of guests he was advised to invite to the wedding breakfast after the ceremony. *Advised* being a gentle word for ordered. A thump sounded from somewhere down the hall, but it barely registered. The servants should be in bed by now, but there was no telling what Mrs. Ferrer had the maids doing these days, especially with the updates being made to the house.

He shifted the papers in his hands to peruse the menu Lady Coyle had devised for the wedding breakfast. Another paper held the address of the church she had deemed appropriate for the ceremony and the minister she believed should officiate. She'd even written vows and detailed how both he and Colleen should be dressed.

He sighed and tossed the lists on his desk before rubbing a hand over his face. If he didn't know better, he would have thought that Lady Coyle was colluding with Fergus to marry off his sisters so that she could organize and direct all of the weddings. The woman had no children of her own, after all, and seemed to take a particularly close interest in the O'Shea family.

Well, so be it. He leaned back in his chair, resting his hands behind his head and closing his eyes. Truly, he didn't care how it happened, he just wanted to have Colleen as his wife. She'd vexed him at every turn, made him roll his eyes and shake his head with her silly carrying-on in town and at events around the county. She amused him, the way one would be amused by a circus act. Or at least she had until a few nights ago.

He exhaled and let his imagination venture off to the fire in her eyes as she'd stood opposite him in his bedroom, undeterred when he'd loosened his robe. He would never forget the touch of her hand gliding over him. Just the thought of it had him straining against his trousers. Her fingers were delicate but strong, and her explorations had been unschooled but bold. He remembered the scent of her skin and the taste of her mouth when he'd kissed her in the hall before that. But it was her emerald-green eyes and the promise they held, the wickedness and the intelligence just waiting to be guided and formed, that had him throbbing. He seriously considered undoing his trousers and relieving himself right there in his office to save him the trouble of heading up to his bedroom. He had a handkerchief on hand and could—

His wicked thoughts were cut short by a horrible, ringing din sounding upstairs. Benedict knew exactly what it was and leapt to his feet, scattering Lady Coyle's papers as he did. He'd set the trap on Quigley's advice as a way to draw the Murphy gang so deep into his house that they wouldn't be able to find their way out before the staff captured and subdued them. In all honesty, Benedict had thought the trap was a foolish diversion, meant to give Quigley and Parsons some time alone, so he'd let the two go ahead and gather every unused pot and pan and crates full of empty tin cans to set the trap. Never in his lifetime would he have imagined the thieves being stupid enough to venture so far into his house. The thought that they'd infiltrated deep into the family quarters had his heart pounding against his ribs as he bounded up the stairs, two and three at a time.

"We caught her, my lord." Parsons greeted him at the

top of the stairs, his expression alight with amusement. "We caught the bloody thief."

"She walked right into the trap, my lord," Quigley added, exchanging a humorous look with Parsons.

"Unhand me!" Colleen shouted as the valet and footman held her in the hall outside of the room where the chest was stored. She struggled and kicked against them, but neither man loosened their grip. "I am not a thief," Colleen insisted. "You are the thief," she hurled at him. "You are the criminal here. You should be ashamed of yourself."

Benedict let out a breath and pinched the bridge of his nose as Colleen continued to struggle against Parsons and Quigley—both of whom seemed to think the situation highly amusing, though they did their best to maintain their dignity, considering it was the sister of an earl they held between them. Worse still, Mr. Conyers, his butler, and Mrs. Ferrers came running down the hall from the servants' stairs, Will, one of the other footmen, racing behind them. And if he wasn't mistaken, Lottie, the scullery maid, was peeking at the scene from around the corner to the grand staircase. His entire household was there to witness Colleen's invasion. By morning, all of County Antrim would know she'd been there. For the second time in a week.

So much for planning a quiet wedding within a reasonable amount of time so as to avoid the hint of scandal.

Benedict squared his shoulders and took a calming

breath before marching down the hall to Colleen. He fixed her with a long, disapproving frown before saying, "You, Lady Colleen, are shredding the last of my nerves." He gestured for Parsons and Quigley to unhand her.

Colleen jerked away from them as they let go. "You are the one who should be upbraided for your crimes," she insisted.

Benedict didn't have the first idea what she was talking about, but if the last few days of their acquaintance had taught him anything, it was that Colleen O'Shea had an imagination that was too vivid to go unchaperoned.

"You can all go," he told his staff. He hoped the look he sent all of them would be enough of a warning for them to stay away, ask no questions, and keep the gossip to a minimum in the morning.

His staff did as they were told, smirking and giving each other knowing looks as they did. Colleen attempted to leave as well, head held high and shoulders pushed back. Benedict caught her wrist and held her to her spot before she could get away.

"Not you," he told her. "You and I have things to talk about."

"I have nothing to say to you, my lord." Colleen attempted to yank out of his grip, but Benedict held fast.

"Perhaps not, but I have plenty to say to you," he said in what he hoped was a dire voice.

Colleen looked suitably intimidated for a few seconds

before assuming a haughty look. "Fine. Say what you need to say, then let me go home."

Benedict laughed ironically. "After this little stunt, my lady, this *is* your home."

"What on earth are you talking about? I—"

Without waiting for her to finish, his hand still clamped around her wrist, Benedict tugged her on down the hall to his bedroom.

"Now wait just one moment," Colleen protested. She tried to dig in her heels, but perhaps not as much as she could have. In fact, she didn't put up much of a resistance at all as he pulled her into his bedroom and shut and locked the door behind her. Only then did he let go of her hand. "This is highly improper and exactly the sort of behavior I would expect from a rogue like you," she said, crossing her arms.

Benedict noted that she didn't scream or call for help, she didn't turn and attempt to flee the room, and she didn't skitter around the edge of his bedroom, attempting to avoid him.

"Do you know what I was doing before you broke into my home, Colleen?" he asked.

"You should not address me by my given name only," she said with more of a pout than he figured she realized.

He ignored her attempt at deflection and went on. "I was sorting through the wedding plans Lady Coyle gave me for our impending nuptials."

"I will not marry you." Colleen glared defiantly at him.

He continued to ignore her. "Lady Coyle's plan was for a Christmas wedding," he went on. "But I think after tonight, I shall look into whatever sort of special license is available these days so that we might be married this weekend."

"What?" Colleen gasped, as though the wind had been knocked out of her.

Benedict made a considering face and an off-hand gesture. "Clearly, you prefer to be at Boleran Hall rather than anywhere else, since this is the second time this week I have caught you slinking through my hallways in the middle of the night dressed in...." He glanced over her person. She was wearing more than a nightgown and robe, but her outfit was little more than a loose blouse and plain skirt. It would take him all of thirty seconds to remove them, which he fully intended to do.

That thought send blood coursing through him, particularly to his cock. Colleen wasn't going to get away with simply stroking him off this time. In fact, if he used his skills well enough, she would drop her objection to their marriage and beg him to marry her the very next day.

That was the plan, but his certainty about it was dented when Colleen growled and said, "I refuse to marry a thief and a gang leader. And as soon as Fergus knows the source of your ill-gotten gains, he will call off the marriage and see that you face the law for what you have done."

He stared at her, trying to decide whether to be more

amused or irritated by her fancies. "What do you imagine I've done now?" he asked.

"You have an entire treasure chest of stolen money in the room next to this one," she said, flinging her arm out to the wall dividing his room from the room where the chest was kept. "And I've put the pieces together. You are the leader of that notorious Murphy gang. No doubt you have been directing them in their thieving ways. The money you are holding is proof of that."

"The money has nothing to do with the Murphy gang," he said. Except, perhaps, his intention to use it as a lure to bring the gang to justice once and for all.

"But you refused to tell me what it was from the other day," Colleen continued to accuse him.

"Because I do not believe it is any of your business," Benedict said.

That only inflamed Colleen's anger. Her eyes widened with indignation. "And that is all you think of women, I suppose. That we should be quiet and stay out of male business. We shouldn't have lives or interests or be curious or creative at all."

"That is not what I believe at all," Benedict said, rubbing a hand over his face, his patience nearing its end. At least he had more of an idea of what was truly behind Colleen's ridiculous fancies and her penchant for getting into trouble in the middle of the night. She was bored with a woman's traditional role, but rather than focusing her energies and efforts on something useful, she was using her imagination to lash out.

"You, sir, are a villain," she went on, pointing at him and seeming to prove his theory. "You are a thief, a leader of thieves. Who knows what other villainy you have perpetrated?" She came closer, close enough to jab her finger against his chest. "Who knows what other crimes you have committed. Perhaps you have kidnapped small children. Perhaps your wife didn't truly die in childbirth. Perhaps you murdered—"

He snatched her hand away from his chest so fast he feared he might have hurt her. "Don't you dare disgrace the memory of that good woman with your antics and your flights of fancy," he hissed, low and dangerous. "Emily was a delicate soul, and she deserves much better than to be disparaged by a disobedient child like you."

"I...I...." Colleen stammered. Every bit of her fury had vanished in an instant, replaced by remorse and guilt, as if she'd snapped out of a trance of her own making. "I'm sorry. I didn't mean to speak ill of her. I'm certain she was a lovely person, and it is a horrible tragedy that she died the way she did." Her voice was small, and tears filled her eyes. "It's not fair. Not at all."

"No, it isn't," Benedict said, softening his voice to match her tone. "Many things in this life are not fair, particularly for women."

She was already nearly flush against him, and he still held her wrist. It was only a quick shift in stance from there to holding her. He slipped his free arm around her back and tugged her close. As soon as he let her wrist go, he moved that hand to cradle the side of her face. He wanted to say a hundred things to her—to commiserate with the fate she was destined to as a woman, to reassure her that he would do his best to make her happy, even though they'd stumbled into their engagement haphazardly. But words didn't feel like the right thing in that moment.

He leaned into her, slanting his mouth over hers and kissing her with all the tenderness he could muster. At first, as he caressed her lips with his own, she made a sound that might have been a protest, but sounded more like pleading to him. He tugged her closer, until her body melded against his, and kissed her more deeply. She opened to him, allowing him to tease his tongue into her mouth and taste her fully.

The sigh that swelled from her was all the signal Benedict needed to know she was his to do with as he pleased. And he intended to do quite a bit to her. Enough to silence her protests, once and for all, and to teach her that there were benefits to being his marchioness. He explored her mouth hungrily, drawing sounds of pleasure from her as he did. He stole a brief glance at her eyes, satisfied when he found them heavy-lidded and unfocused. A smile played across his mouth before he dove in for more kisses. She wouldn't protest what they were about to do at all. In fact, he hoped she directed all of the energy she'd spent fighting him into making love to him.

There was only one way to find out. He pulled the hem of her blouse from the waist of her skirt and smoothed his hand up the trim lines of her corset to one breast. The damnable garment kept him from doing more than caressing her trapped breast. He refused to be blocked from what he wanted, so he shifted his hands to undo the row of buttons at the front of her blouse, stealing kisses as he did, then went straight to work unhooking her corset.

Once it was loose, he was able to reach inside to take a much larger handful of her ample breast. She was exquisitely shaped, more than a handful, with large nipples that he could see through the thin fabric of her chemise. Those nipples were already pert, but he rubbed and teased them until they were hard pebbles.

"Oh," Colleen sighed, tilting her head back slightly. It was clear as day she enjoyed the sensations he caused.

Her enjoyment made him as hard as iron. His energy shifted from teasing lightly to wanting to be naked with her as quickly as possible. He went to work removing her blouse and corset entirely, unhooking her skirt in the process and pushing it down her legs. He thanked God she was wearing simple clothes instead of a more ornate cage of a dress. He was able to undress her entirely and carry her to his bed within a minute.

As he laid her across his bedcovers then stepped back to shed his own clothes at lightning speed, Colleen seemed to come out of her desire-induced trance. "Oh!" she gasped, glancing down at herself first before snapping her head up to watch him. "This is quite a bit more than what happened the other night."

Benedict had his shirt off, his trousers unfastened,

and was leaning over to pull his shoes off as she made her comment. He tugged one shoe off, balancing precariously as he glanced at her from his awkward position, and said, "I intend to make love to you. I have no intention of holding back. If that is not what you want, I suggest you gather your things and flee as quickly as possible. Because once I start, I do not plan to stop." It was a bit of a lie. He would stop fully if she changed her mind at any point. But instinct told him that it would be better to issue an ultimatum to Colleen than to be vague in any way.

"Um...." She hesitated, biting her lip and squirming on his bed in a way that did nothing for Benedict's resolve to be as much of a gentleman as possible. Her hips were creamy and shapely, her thighs beckoned to him, and the thatch of curls between her legs was a soft shade of cinnamon that he was dying to explore. He pulled off his remaining shoe and straightened, well aware that the evidence of his arousal was on full display with his trousers undone. Her gaze focused in on him there. "Well, all right, then. If you insist," she said breathlessly.

Benedict was tempted to laugh, but other things tempted him more. He shucked his trousers, grinning at the way she gasped as his cock sprung free and stood up, stiff and proud. He let her look as he moved slowly to the bed and threw aside some of the pillows at its head, then peeled down the bedclothes. Colleen scurried over those bedclothes, repositioning herself between his sheets. Her movements were stilted and uncertain, as though she wanted to know what she was doing but didn't.

"Do you trust me?" Benedict asked, climbing into bed.

"No," she said honestly. "Not one bit." She swallowed. "But go ahead."

He smiled in spite of himself. She was darling, when it came down to it. And she might not have thought that she trusted him, but the way she let him handle her and lay her on her back, then nestle between her legs told a different story.

He rewarded her for her trust by showering her with kisses—first to her lips and cheeks, then in a trail down her neck, and then across her breasts. She made a charmingly erotic sound of surprise and delight as he licked her hardened nipples, then teased them with his teeth, then suckled her mercilessly. Her body writhed against his, and she arched into him, unable to catch her breath.

"No one told me it would be like this," she gasped as he nudged her thighs farther apart, his hands roving her hips and stomach as though he could feel all of her at once.

"What did they tell you it would be like?" he asked, lifting to look into her eyes for a moment.

"No one tells women anything," she sighed in irritation. "Even Marie wasn't detailed enough in her descriptions of the marriage bed."

"She wasn't?" Benedict could barely hide his amusement as he brushed his hand lightly over her stomach and hip, over the outside of her thigh, then up her inner thigh.

"Not at all," she huffed. "Though after I told her

about touching your member the other day, she said I should just wait and see how lovely it is to taste it."

Benedict nearly came undone then and there. The very thought of Colleen swallowing him brought him so close to the edge that he had to steady his breathing and will himself not to come. There would be plenty of time for every sort of exploration later, but if he didn't bury himself within her and let her heat and tightness do the trick for him—which he fully intended to do, like an absolute rake—he might go mad.

"Did your sister tell you about this?" he asked.

Colleen started to answer, "No," before he brought his hand up to tease and stroke her wetness. And she was dripping wet. Her answer turned into a long, surprised sigh as he circled her slick heat with his fingertips, teasing her open, and attempting to ascertain just how much pain she might feel in a moment. He was no expert, but he was reasonably certain she was still intact. Better still, the way she caught her breath and gasped for more as he tested her with one, two, then three fingers, hinted that they could probably skate through the inevitable breeching with relative ease.

"Nice, isn't it?" he teased her like a rogue, thrusting with his fingers before shifting so that he could rub her clit with his thumb.

"Nice isn't the word for—oh!"

He must have stroked her exactly right. She bucked against his hand, panting vocally. Better still, she moved with him, instinctively attempting to bring herself to orgasm by grinding against his hand and thumb.

Orgasm was exactly what she achieved mere seconds later. Benedict cursed under his breath at the unfettered way she cried out as her inner muscles throbbed around his fingers. He wanted to feel all of that and more with his cock. Without waiting, hoping she would be so distracted with pleasure she wouldn't feel a moment of pain, he shifted over her. Hoping it would help ease things, he parted her legs more, then thrust into her.

It was the single most enjoyable moment of his life. She felt so perfect and tight around him. His whole body cried out in triumph as he sank deep inside of her. He tried to pause, tried to listen for any indication that she was uncomfortable, but his driving need made it difficult to focus on anything but moving within her. She felt so good that he was certain he'd lose his mind.

That amazing feeling turned to absolute bliss as she circled her arms and legs around him. The moment he realized the sounds she made weren't yelps of pain but cries of ecstasy was perfect. He let himself go, then, moving hard and fast, reveling in the way pleasure built up—like white-hot fire—inside of him. He wanted her, all of her. He wanted to claim her and spill inside of her and make her his forever. So much that he made sounds that he'd never made with a woman before, baring himself to her in a thousand ways.

At last, he came with startling force. It felt as though his life and soul poured into her in a dazzling burst of pleasure. It felt so good that the world ceased to exist for a moment. There was only him and her and pleasure and happiness. It was so much that, as soon as he was spent, he didn't even have the energy to pull out of her right away. He simply lay there, hoping he wasn't crushing her, but without the wherewithal to do anything about it.

"That was...." Colleen panted, but didn't finish her sentence.

"You see?" he asked, finally gathering the strength to roll to the side. He didn't have more energy than that, though. The sleep that inevitably encompassed him after sex was already settling in. He flailed for Colleen, drawing her close. He was shocked when she actually snuggled against him, her hot, damp body feeling perfect against his.

"Well, I suppose that is worth the price of marriage," she said, resting her head against his shoulder. "If that's what it means to be your marchioness—"

Her words were cut short—as was the heated peace enveloping them—by an almighty crash downstairs.

CHAPTER 8

*S*tunned. Amazed. Tingly. Delighted.

Those were just a few of the words Colleen could think of to describe what she and Lord Boleran—blast it, she should probably call him Benedict now, after all that—had done. Invasive, overwhelming, and erotic were words that came to mind as well. It had all felt so wonderful, even though Benedict had mastered her the entire time. Several pieces of things Marie had told her or bits she'd learned herself over the years had suddenly come together to form a complete picture in her mind that had her thinking, "Ah! That's what it's all about," even as her body was crying out, "*Aaah! That's what it's all* about!"

On top of that, thanks to her experience with Benedict's member a few nights before, she was well aware that he'd exploded inside of her. She could feel remnants of his fluid tickling her inner thigh as she'd snuggled against him, resting her head on his broad, delicious shoulder. A few more pieces of the matrimonial puzzle fit together in her mind, and she realized that was how women became pregnant. It had to be.

There was no getting out of it now. She would have to marry Benedict. Even if he was a highwayman on his way to the gallows, Fergus wouldn't let her back out now. And if she were honest with herself, she didn't think she wanted to.

"Well, I suppose that is worth the price of marriage." She snuggled against Benedict's strong, overheated form, scrambling for a way to give in to other people's machinations for her without losing face. "If that's what it means to be your marchioness—"

As soon as the crash sounded from downstairs, she snapped straight, her heart racing so fast she couldn't breathe. Benedict sat bolt-upright as well. When he did, Colleen gasped so hard she started coughing and gathered the bedclothes around her chest.

"What was that?" she asked through her coughing as Benedict scrambled out of bed. For a man who had been dozing off just moments before, he had quite a bit of fire in him all of a sudden.

"I don't know," he said as he dashed around his room, picking his discarded clothes off the floor and dressing.

All Colleen could think was that Fergus had found her out. She imagined her brother had discovered her missing from her room at Dunegard Castle, had marched all the way to Boleran Hall, and would drag her and Benedict down to the vicarage that very night to be wed.

A split-second later, she realized how ridiculous the idea was. Not only was poor Fergus no longer capable of marching anywhere to do anything, he'd already won his gamble. She and Benedict would definitely be married.

She shuffled to the edge of the bed, self-conscious about her debauched state, but got up anyhow, dressing again the way Benedict was dressing. The rest of the house wasn't as silent as she'd hoped it would be, considering what she and Benedict had ended up doing. Benedict had sent his servants to bed, but they were most definitely up and dashing around the house again. At least, that was who she hoped was making the racket and shouting downstairs.

"You should stay here," Benedict said once he was fully dressed. He raced to his bedroom door and unlocked it. "It might not be safe."

"I will do no such thing," Colleen insisted, marching to the door to join him.

Benedict shifted to bar the way, his back to the door for a moment. He opened his mouth as if he would order her back to bed, but sense seemed to get the better of him. He pressed his lips shut and blew out a breath through his nose. "Even if I leave you here," he said, "you're just going to follow me the second I've turned my back on you."

"Why, Benedict," Colleen said with a smile. "I'd no idea you were such a quick study."

His wry smile turned suddenly soft and sentimental. "You just called me Benedict," he said. His voice had gone deliciously tender as well.

"Of course, I did," Colleen said. She blinked at him, her heart swelling and filling with warmth the way other parts of her had when she'd been lying under him. Benedict didn't actually care for her, did he? As more than just an irritating bedmate and future piece of property?

Another thump sounded from downstairs. That ended any argument or discussion she and Benedict might have had. Benedict moved aside and threw open the door. He took her hand as they dashed into the hall. At first, Colleen thought it was a lovely, tender show of support. When they reached the top of the grand staircase and he used his grip on her hand to hold her back when she started to charge ahead of him down the stairs, she realized his grasp on her was as much to keep her behind him as it was a show of affection.

That left her frustrated and fuming all over again by the time they made it to the bottom of the stairs.

"What happened?" Benedict asked as they met up with the valet and the footman in the large front hall.

Colleen noted with a startled blink that the two men were utterly disheveled, with their shirts unbuttoned, and Mr. Quigley had a fresh, red mark on his neck. "Were you attacked?" she asked, anxious for the two young men.

For some reason, the two looked guilty at her question. They glanced to each other and blushed, stammering without answering. Finally, Mr. Parsons shook his head and focused on Benedict. "It was the Murphy gang, my lord," he said. "It had to be. They came in through one of the doors in the conservatory."

"I came in through a door in the conservatory," Colleen said. Now she was the one who felt guilty. She should have locked the door behind her when she entered. But then again, why had it been unlocked in the first place?

"I should have been paying more attention," Mr. Quigley said, looking a different sort of guilty. He peeked at Mr. Parsons, then sent a deeply apologetic look to Benedict. "The plan was to give them a way to get in, then to monitor them as they made their way up to Lord O'Shea's money."

"Good Lord, that money belongs to Fergus?" Colleen thumped a hand to her chest, stunned by the turn of events. A moment later, she blinked. Had Fergus paid Benedict that sum of money to take her off his hands?

Benedict cleared up her confusion and stopped her imagination from spinning yet another wild tale by saying, "It's your cousin, Cailean O'Shea's money."

"Oh." Colleen blinked. "Then you should call him Lord Dervock, not Lord O'Shea. He's Viscount Dervock from our uncle's side, you see, and—"

"I do appreciate this lesson in family connections, Colleen," Benedict cut her off, "and you can educate me in full later. But for now...." He turned back to his footman and valet—who had busied themselves tucking in their shirts and fastening their waistcoats while

Colleen had been speaking. Though why the thieves had thought to attempt to undress the two men was a mystery to her. "I take it your plan to lie in wait in the conservatory until the thieves broke in didn't go as planned?" Benedict asked them. He arched one eyebrow and crossed his arms, rather like a teacher facing two children who had deliberately gotten into trouble.

"I...I understand if you wish to terminate my employment, my lord," Mr. Parsons muttered. He glanced to Mr. Quigley.

"As do I, my lord." Mr. Quigley lowered his head.

"Lucky for the both of you, I have no intention of sacking you," Benedict said. "But you're a danger to yourselves and each other. Now, go on up to bed—separately —before Mr. Conyers drags his tired old bones down here to see what is the matter. We'll discuss ways to keep the two of you from being thrown in prison in the morning."

Mr. Parsons and Mr. Quigley exchanged utterly startled looks. Colleen was decidedly perplexed as well. If it were her home, she would have been furious that the two men who had said they would stand guard and watch for robbers had failed in their efforts, been attacked, and nearly humiliated in the process.

"Thank you, my lord," both Mr. Quigley and Mr. Parsons said, bowing and nodding in disbelief as they hurried out of the room and on their way.

Benedict shook his head and rubbed a hand over his face before marching across the conservatory to check the doors. "It was only a matter of time," he muttered, opening one of the French doors and looking outside to the garden. "I'll have to keep both of them on indefinitely now, if only to stop the two of them from being arrested. Though they'll work harder in thanks. God help me if they have a falling out."

He could have been speaking in Hindustani, for all Colleen understood his words. "Will you please explain to me what is going on?" she asked, taking a step toward him.

Benedict shut the French door and strode toward her. "With Quigley and Parsons? Absolutely not," he said adamantly. "You may be progressive, my sweet, but there are some things even a modern woman should not know."

Colleen's mind scattered in two directions at once. He'd called her by a term of endearment, and, Lord help her, she'd actually liked it. But to declare there were some things she should not know? Unforgiveable.

"Why would you send Mr. Quigley and Mr. Parsons to prison for failing to prevent thieves from breeching your house?" she demanded. "In fact, they prevented any sort of theft from happening. They fought the thieves off before they could advance into any other part of the house, and Mr. Quigley sustained a wound on his neck as proof of that. If you ask me, you should be thanking them instead of scolding them."

Benedict simply stared at her, mouth hanging open, amusement in his eyes. The man had some gall to be *amused* by her observations and her defense of the poor footman and valet.

Benedict cleared his throat and stood straighter. "My dear, it was Quigley and Parsons's idea to leave a door open for thieves and to lure them into the house so they could be captured in the first place. I considered the idea ridiculous, and I suspected—as, indeed, has been proven accurate—that the scheme was more of an excuse for the two of them to—" He shook his head and paced around the room, his expression falling into a frown. "Part of the idea was making known that Cailean's chest was being stored in an upstairs room in my house. It seems as though that fact actually reached the ears of the Murphy gang. I shouldn't have let the farce go as far as it did, but those two work so hard and have so little opportunity to—"

Colleen let out an impatient breath. She was exceedingly weary of the way Benedict kept cutting himself off, just when she thought his words might actually begin to make sense and form a complete thought. "If you're upset about Mr. Quigley and Mr. Parsons luring the Murphy gang to your house to steal Cousin Cailean's money, then why not just sack them?"

Benedict snapped his eyes up to meet hers. "Because I have a burden of care when it comes to the people whose lives and livelihoods fall within my provenance," he said. "Be they my staff or my family. I take that burden of care seriously. If those two were to be left to their own devices—" He snapped his mouth shut and shook his head.

Colleen growled in frustration, close to tearing her

hair out. "I demand you tell me everything that is going on this instant. Why do you have a chest of money belonging to Cousin Cailean in your possession? Why do you have his glider in your barn, for that matter? What does the plan of your footman and your valet to capture the Murphy gang have to do with anything at all under the sun? And for God's sake, why didn't you just explain everything to me from the start so that I wouldn't feel the need to sneak over here in the dead of night to uncover the truth for myself?"

"Because none of these matters should be your concern at all," Benedict said, changing direction in his pacing to march up to her. "Women need not concern themselves with money. Your cousin entrusted me with a sum, and that is all you need know. Aeronautics are a man's field as well. Your cousin's glider is none of your concern. And I'll be damned if I explain so much as a hint of what Quigley and Parsons were up to this evening."

Colleen was so frustrated with his boorish masculinity that she wanted to shout. Or cry. "Oh, yes," she raged, dripping with sarcasm. "We cannot trust women with anything half as important as money or machinery or robbers at all. Women are too weak to withstand it. We would collapse into a pile of ashes if even a bit of responsibility were given to us."

"That is not at all what I mean, Colleen," Benedict said in a dark voice.

"It is," she insisted. "It is so much a part of what you

111

mean that you don't even see it. You are so confirmed in your prejudiced ways that you don't realize your own prejudice, but that's what it is."

"I will not put you at risk—either physically or spiritually—by exposing you to the machinations of a gang of thieves. Or the relations of young men," Benedict boomed, towering over her.

"Yes, because the entire world would come to an end if women were anything less than perfectly safe or perfectly innocent," Colleen shot back at him. "Please do not curse me with perfection. Treasures are always more precious when they are slightly tarnished." Benedict opened his mouth to speak, but Colleen rode over him with, "If you did not think so, you would not have bedded me this evening."

Benedict's mouth snapped shut, and he rocked back. He regarded Colleen as though she might actually have made a good point. The surge of victory Colleen had at his reaction pushed her on.

"You say I am to be your marchioness, my lord—" she took a step toward him, and Benedict actually stepped back, "—but if you want to be my marquess, I demand that you treat me as your equal."

"Colleen, I don't think that's—"

"You've made quite certain that there is no backing out of this marriage now," Colleen went on. "But if you want to have any sort of a caring relationship with me, any sort of connection built on friendship and mutual respect, you will have to stop treating me as though I am some silly child and bring me into the inner circle of your thoughts. If you do, you might just discover that there is more to the modern woman than embroidery and tea parties."

"I do know that there is more to women these days than—"

Colleen held up a finger to stop him from going on. "I demand respect, Benedict. If this is to be my fate, then I need you to listen to me. If you did, you might just discover that I have ideas of my own. Ideas that might help you run an unruly household. Ideas about money born of my sisters' brewing business. Ideas about how to capture a gang of thieves. You will never discover any of that if you persist in being a callous, wicked, insufferable, unfeeling...." She took a breath.

"Have you run out of words yet?" Benedict asked in a flat voice.

"I am merely restocking the stores of my vocabulary," Colleen seethed.

"Well, when you've found a few other words to let me know what a sorry specimen of manliness I am, be sure to tell me."

He stepped forward, taking her hand and leading her out to the hall.

"Where are we going?" Colleen asked, tempted to resist him to prove a point, but also curious about what might happen if they returned to his bedroom.

"To bed," he said, seeming to confirm her suspicions. A thrill of anticipation shot through her, but Benedict squelched it with a look. "To sleep," he emphasized. "God only knows how exhausted I am at this point."

"Yes, you are rather exhausting," Colleen said in a wry voice, mounting the stairs with him.

He glared at her, but the energy quickly drained from his look. "We're going to sleep," he said. "And yes, you are sleeping in my bed. I see no point in rousing any of the maids to prepare a guest room for you, particularly as, once I return you to your brother tomorrow—for the second time in a week—he and Lady Coyle will insist we are wed post haste. We'll be sharing a bed nightly for the rest of our lives by the weekend anyhow. We might as well get used to it."

Colleen thought about protesting, but found that she didn't really want to. The fight had gone out of her. In no way whatsoever would she be able to wiggle out of marrying Benedict now. And if she were honest with herself, she didn't want to. At the same time, no matter what Benedict wanted, she refused to be belittled.

CHAPTER 9

*I*n spite of everything, Benedict slept well through the night. Perhaps it was the feeling that he was ready to utterly wash his hands of all the nonsense taking place in his household and simply let his staff and his future wife run wild. In truth, he knew he could do no such thing, particularly with the Murphy gang still on the loose. Whatever Parsons and Quigley's plan had actually been intended to accomplish, Benedict was certain the real thieves had made an astoundingly bold attempt to break into his house the night before.

He shouldn't have slept a wink. Shouldn't have, except the other reason his body had given up and his mind had drifted away into the ether was underscored by waking up with Colleen tucked against his side. The mad creature was fully dressed in her simple blouse and skirt, and even though she had fallen asleep with her back to him at the far edge of his bed late in the night they'd just endured, there she was in the morning, one leg hitched over his thigh, her cheek nestled against his shoulder, her arm thrown over his chest.

Benedict smiled. A man could get used to waking up in such a way. For more reasons than merely the intensity of his morning wood—which he knew he wouldn't be able to do anything about, because Colleen would likely fly into a rage the moment she awoke. In sleep, Colleen betrayed the feelings that she fought so hard to hide in the daylight. She wanted comfort and closeness. She wanted to be cherished and included. Emily hadn't been like that at all. Emily had known her duty, and her every waking moment had been devoted to carrying out that duty, independent of anything to do with him.

Yes, Colleen was certainly different. Benedict shifted slightly, rolling to his side and gathering her into his arms as gently as he could so as not to wake her too fast. He had the feeling she was far better suited to him and would make him far happier than Emily had, God rest the woman's soul. His problem was that he had no idea how to proceed from where they were. He was baffled at the prospect of finding a way to fulfill the demands she'd made in such a temper the night before while being a good, protective husband. As determined as Colleen was, she most definitely needed someone to guide her and keep her from doing herself harm.

She drew in a breath and started to come out of sleep at last. The way she stretched against him did nothing for the self-control Benedict knew he had to maintain. Her body was a garden of wonders that he'd only begun to explore. And her sleepy smile as she blinked open bleary eyes and gazed straight into his filled his heart with joy and excitement.

"Good morning," he said in a deep, hushed voice.

"Good morning," she sighed in return, continuing to stretch with contentment, driving him wild as her leg brushed against his straining cock. She caught her breath and her eyes went wide, likely realizing her situation at last, then hissed, "No!"

She sat up, pushing away from Benedict and scrambling out the far side of the bed. Benedict breathed out in disappointment, flopping to his back. It wasn't as though he hadn't expected her reaction, but it was a disappointment all the same.

"This is intolerable," Colleen went on, hopping around the room as she gathered her corset, chemise, shoes, and stockings. "I should have insisted you have a guestroom prepared for me. I never intended to spend the night all—" She gestured to him, but her movements and her jaw went slack as Benedict peeled back the covers, revealing his bare chest and tented pajamas.

He was in no mood for an argument. If he'd had his way, he would have spent the morning making love to Colleen before returning her to her brother. But that was as impossible as presenting Colleen to Queen Victoria as a model of grace and virtue.

"Would you like to use the chamber pot first, or shall I?" he asked, as banal as possible. Perhaps the strategy he should employ with Colleen going forward was not to rise to her challenges. At least, not that sort of rising and not that sort of challenge. "My apologies for not having modern plumbing facilities installed at Boleran Hall as of yet. I have been working with the county on ordinances to install pipes and other necessities throughout my property, but as there is such a high demand for updates these days, and a few structural changes are in process to prepare for it, that it has been a slow process."

Colleen merely stared at him, her eyes narrowed suspiciously. He'd droned on about pipes purposely— another strategy he might try more often to neutralize her misplaced anger. Perhaps he could bore the vinegar out of her.

"If...if you could wait a minute...I truly do need to go," she mumbled, lowering her head slightly and looking sheepish.

The moment she ducked behind the screen in the corner of his room, Benedict indulged in a smile. So there were ways to soothe the savage vixen that was Colleen O'Shea. He would remember that. But he had a long, long way to go before the woman did anything but make his head spin.

They washed and dressed with far less ceremony or importance than the previous morning Colleen had spent at his house. Or so he assumed, considering he hadn't been privy to her morning ablutions earlier in the week. Colleen didn't have fresh clothing to change into, like she had then. When they made their way down to the breakfast room, every servant they passed—with the obvious exceptions of Quigley and Parsons—was surprised to see them together. Or perhaps simply surprised that what they'd seen the night before, when Colleen set off the makeshift alarm in the room with Cailean's money, had truly happened instead of being something they'd all imagined.

Breakfast was a swift affair as well, and before nine, Benedict and Colleen were riding back to Dunegard Castle in an almost comedic repeat of the journey they'd made days before.

"You aren't going to get away with this," Colleen said as they started up the gravel drive to the castle's front door.

Benedict laughed, lounging against his seat. "What, precisely, do you think I am attempting to get away with?" he asked. He was far more at ease than he had been the first time he'd delivered Colleen home after an unscheduled night at his house. He was already engaged to her, and after the night they'd spent, anything that would see them to the altar faster was a blessing. He didn't even mind the hint of scandal that would come with a rushed wedding now.

Colleen's brow darkened. "I know what kind of man you are, Benedict."

"Do you?" he asked, arching one eyebrow casually.

"Yes. You are a rake and a rogue. You care for no one but yourself. You are harboring those thieves somehow, and you will keep me a virtual prisoner in your home once we are wed, I just know it." She narrowed her eyes even further.

Benedict was too bemused by the sullen way she'd delivered her diatribe—which was a sharp contrast to the flames of her anger in the days before—to do anything but chuckle fondly. "My dear, you do not know me at all. Fortunately, time and proximity will change that."

She didn't have a chance to refute him. The carriage lurched to a stop just outside of Dunegard Castle's front door. The skies above were gray, and already, rain spit down on them, so they didn't dawdle as they climbed out of the carriage. Colleen didn't even try to pull away as he rested a hand on the small of her back and rushed her into her brother's house.

The entire family was assembled in the breakfast room as the butler showed them in. Colleen's sisters exclaimed in relief at the sight of her and leapt up from their chairs to embrace her. Fergus and his wife—the incomparable and charming Lady Henrietta—exchanged sly and knowing looks. If Benedict didn't know better, he would have thought the two had had a bet about where Colleen was and in what manner she would return home.

"Lord O'Shea." Benedict bowed with exaggerated formality as Colleen sent him a scathing look and moved to the side with her sisters. "Once again, I have returned your prodigal sister to the bosom of her family."

"Do I want to know how she ended up in your possession again?" Fergus asked from the head of the breakfast table, sending Colleen a teasing smile.

"No, you do not," Colleen said with an air of finality, tilting her chin up.

"Your sister cannot resist my company," Benedict said. She would hate him for it, but he was too charmed by her irascible behavior to let the whole thing go. "It seems she would much rather be at Boleran Hall than Dunegard Castle."

"I would not," Colleen protested.

Benedict ignored her, going on with, "Therefore, my lord, I would suggest that we rearrange plans for the wedding so that it might take place as soon as possible." He sent Fergus a look that he hoped the man would understand as the true reason they needed to hasten things.

Fergus nodded slowly, grinning, and shook his head. "Forgive me if I don't call you out for besmirching my sister's honor," he laughed. "Chances are Colleen will avenge herself."

"Indeed." Benedict laughed along with him.

"This is no laughing matter," Colleen said with a sniff. "The two of you are horrid. I am going to my room to wash this entire wretched night away and forget the lot of you exist."

She marched out of the room, head held high. Her sisters watched her go before returning to their seats at the breakfast table, rightfully stunned. Benedict remained where he was for a moment.

"Before I go," he said, eyeing the ladies at the table anxiously, "there are a few matters I wish to discuss with you, Fergus."

"About my sister?" Fergus looked as though they would be discussing Doomsday.

Benedict tilted his head to the side with a sheepish look. "That, but one other thing. About the recent string of thefts in the county."

"Oh, that." Fergus took a sip from the cup of coffee he'd picked up as Benedict was talking, then gestured to one of the free chairs. "Join us for the remainder of the meal. We'll adjourn to my study afterwards."

Benedict nodded and helped himself not only to the offered chair, but coffee as well. He felt far more at ease at the O'Shea's table than he probably had any right to, but they would all be family sooner rather than later. It would be good for Colleen if he fit in as one of her own.

COLLEEN WASHED AND CHANGED INTO A CLEAN DAY dress as soon as she reached her room. She wanted to be furious over everything that had happened, but in truth, her heart was so tangled with conflicting emotions that she didn't know what she wanted anymore. The only reason she'd argued with Benedict that morning or protested in the breakfast room was because that was what she always did. That was what she felt she had to do to be who she was.

Now, she wasn't as certain. Yes, she was a strong woman, capable of writing her own destiny. But as she walked down the stairs with the intent of rejoining her sisters—wherever they were and whatever activity they had in store for the day—she wasn't certain that the way she'd taken command of her life before was the same way she should take command of her life going forward. The life of an independent spinster that she'd always assumed she would live was vastly different than the life of a marchioness.

And then there was Benedict. Vile and stubborn though he was, she had to admit that there would be certain charms to being married to the man. He was handsome to a fault, and her body still felt the imprint of him. Bedsport was just the sort of wickedness she could get used to. If only he wasn't such a horrid person.

But was he, really? Could she, as his marchioness, find a way to straighten and correct him? How much sway did wives truly have with their husbands after all?

She needed to speak with Marie. Even though she hadn't been married to Lord Kilrea long, Marie would know the answer to the question of whether wives could change their husbands. She altered her path through the house, heading down the long hall that would take her out a side door so that she could retrieve her bicycle—which had, once again, been returned to Dunegard Castle strapped to the back of Benedict's carriage.

Her path took her past Fergus's office, and she stopped dead when she heard Benedict's voice from within.

"...and with the Murphy gang growing bolder, I fear

for the safety of my tenants and my household," Benedict said.

Colleen caught her breath, pressing her back against the wall just outside of Fergus's office.

"I hate the fact that there's nothing I can do to track those Murphys down myself and bring them to justice," Fergus growled. "Those blackguards are the worst sort of men, attacking those who are trying to help people and lift them up."

"I was able to offer a donation to Arthur O'Neill after the Murphys robbed him on his way back from the livestock auction," Benedict went on. "O'Neill is a proud man, but he accepted the help."

"That was kind of you," Fergus said. "A farmer like O'Neill could be ruined without the money from a livestock sale."

"I just wish there was more that I could do to bring these men to justice." Colleen was surprised at the genuine feeling in Benedict's voice. She hadn't thought him capable of feeling at all. "We know who the men are. It infuriates me that there are others out there helping to hide them."

"That's why they need to be caught red-handed," Fergus said.

"And I've tried. Believe me, I've tried." Benedict let out a breath. He must have been pacing. He came so close to the doorway that Colleen held her breath and pressed hard into the wall, praying he didn't see or hear her. "Some of my household attempted to lure them into revealing themselves last night," he went on, pacing back toward Fergus's desk, or so Colleen assumed. "Though, to be honest, I didn't think Quigley and Parsons were truly attempting to catch thieves at all."

"What do you mean?" Fergus asked.

Benedict chuckled warily. "They were trying to catch each other. The two have been sweet on each other almost from the moment I hired Parsons."

Colleen's eyes snapped wide. Mr. Parsons and Mr. Quigley were sweet on each other? Two men? But that was...that was illegal, for one.

Benedict's comment about needing to keep them on out of fear of them being arrested suddenly made sense.

"And you haven't sacked one or both of them?" Fergus asked, mirroring her train of thought somewhat. He sounded amused, which surprised Colleen.

"God, no," Benedict replied. "Quigley and Parsons are young and in love. Can you imagine what they would be up against, out there in the world, if I sacked them? Their sort of love might not be approved of by society, but, call me sentimental, I cannot, in good conscience, deny two young people what their hearts want. I couldn't be so cruel. The two will have places and a home under my roof for as long as they would like, provided they are discreet." He paused. "I feel as though it is my duty to protect the souls entrusted to my care with everything I have."

Colleen pressed a hand to her chest, surprised to find her heart thumping furiously. She'd always been given to understand that aberrations like Mr. Quigley and Mr. Parsons should be shunned, but she'd rather liked both men, from what little she knew of them. It was almost... almost *noble* of Benedict to care for them so when his own reputation would be at risk, should they expose themselves. And Benedict had given money to a farmer who was robbed by the Murphy gang?

"Which brings me around to the other matter I wish to discuss with you," Benedict went on.

"My sister?" Fergus guessed.

"Your sister," Benedict repeated. Colleen fancied that she could hear the smile in his voice. "She's lovely, Fergus. She's a minx and a hellion, but she's lovely."

Colleen's brow shot up, and her heart squeezed even harder. Benedict thought she was lovely?

Fergus laughed. "I'm glad you feel that way, man. Because you're the one who's going to be stuck with her for the rest of your natural days."

"And I'm glad of it," Benedict went on, making Colleen's heart squeeze even more. "Colleen is lively and interesting. I have a feeling she will keep me on my toes once we are married. Which, I might add, I truly would like to have happen as soon as possible."

"That can be arranged," Fergus said. "I'm certain Lady Coyle will be beside herself to have all her grand plans cast aside in favor of a scandalously rushed wedding."

"Lady Coyle can go fuck herself," Benedict said.

Colleen nearly gave herself away by gulping with

sudden laughter. She slapped a hand to her mouth to keep the sound contained. So that was how men spoke to each other when they were alone, eh?

"It is not the wedding I am concerned with, it's after," Benedict went on.

"I take it you're not talking about the wedding night," Fergus said, his tone amused. "I don't want to know the slightest detail about you bedding my sister."

"And I would never reveal anything half so intimate," Benedict laughed. He cleared his throat and went on with, "What I am concerned with is how to manage her once we are married."

Anger pulsed suddenly through Colleen, replacing the warm feelings that had seeped in around her edges as she let her guard down. Of course, Benedict wanted to *manage* her.

But she had a hard time holding onto her anger when Benedict went on with, "Colleen spoke frankly with me last night, and I was deeply impressed by what she said. I believe she has it within her to be a powerful force in the county and in Ireland, both personally and where the advancement of women is concerned. But she is so impulsive, so rash in her actions."

Colleen's heart hurdled toward anger again, but her mind stopped her. She *had* been rash. She *was* impulsive. Otherwise, she wouldn't have ended up in the mess she was in.

"I would like your advice," Benedict went on, his tone making it sound as though he'd reached his point, "on how to best encourage Colleen's strengths while lifting her out of her weaknesses."

Something tender overrode any remaining anger Colleen felt. That was what Benedict wanted? That was...that was almost sweet.

Fergus laughed. "If I knew how to tame my sisters while still allowing them to flourish, I would write a book about it and earn enough money to relax for the rest of my life."

"You have had your hands full," Benedict said.

"And my hands are one of the few parts of me that still work perfectly after that wretched attack."

Colleen's heart bled for her brother. He truly deserved better than to be a cripple for the rest of his life.

"I've learned a lot from being married to a strong woman myself," Fergus went on. "The very best piece of advice I can give you is this. Never, ever underestimate a woman. And never fall prey to the myth so many like to hurl from the pulpit that women are a weaker sex or that their minds are fragile. That's all tripe. Always treat your wife as though the next thing to issue forth from her beautiful lips is the advice you will need to solve all of your problems."

"What a lovely thought," Benedict said. Colleen frowned, trying to determine if he was speaking sarcastically, but she didn't think he was.

"Talk to her," Fergus went on. "As often as possible. Confide in your wife, and let her confide in you. That's the only way to avoid misunderstandings."

"This all sounds like sound and reasonable advice," Benedict said. "I shall most certainly take it under advisement." He paused for a moment. Colleen heard movement from the office before Benedict went on with, "And now, I'll have to take my leave of you. I'm expecting your cousin, Cailean, later this morning. He hinted to me that it will take the bank in Belfast much longer to retrieve his money from the land sale than he'd previously anticipated, so it's likely that your sister will be forced to think I'm a thief and a pirate for days or weeks more."

Fergus laughed. Colleen didn't find the situation as amusing. At the same time, she wasn't angry. She sensed she was close to being discovered eavesdropping, so she fled down the hall the way she'd come. Her mind spun in circles, and she barely saw where she was going. She'd been wrong about nearly everything she thought she believed about Benedict, and now she didn't know what to do.

CHAPTER 10

"Colleen! You look as though you've seen a ghost."

Chloe's call from the sisters' parlor snapped Colleen out of the muddle of her thoughts. She was grateful to have something to ground and focus her, and veered into the parlor. As soon as Shannon and Chloe saw her, they stood from where they had been lounging on the parlor's sofas, playing some sort of card game—no doubt one of the mad ones that they'd all made up while living at the cottage.

"I haven't seen a ghost," Colleen said, letting her sisters lead her to one of the sofas.

"A demon then. It was that horrible Lord Boleran, wasn't it?" Shannon asked as she and Chloe sat on either side of Colleen. "He kept you a prisoner in his house last night and did unspeakable things to you, didn't he?"

Colleen sent Shannon a sheepish look. "I would not

speak of the things he did to me, no," she said carefully. "But I wouldn't call them horrible."

Both Shannon and Chloe gaped at her, pink flooding their cheeks.

"Did he...that is to say...*did he?*" Chloe gasped, her eyes going as wide as Colleen had ever seen them.

Colleen let her thoughts drift as she slumped as far as her corset would allow her. Going to bed with Benedict had been the best part of her evening. The whole experience had been so new and so exciting. She should have been frightened and overwhelmed by his size and the unfamiliarity of his body and everything he'd done to her. But as her memory of his kisses returned, she felt herself flush with remembered passion. The way he had touched her everywhere, the expertise of his mouth on her body, the pure pleasure he had conjured up in her had been lovely in every way.

Lovely, just like Benedict had just said she was. He'd said such wonderful things to Fergus. Wonderful things not just about her, but about the people he felt responsible for.

"I think I have made a grave miscalculation," she said, her voice little more than a hoarse whisper.

Shannon frowned. "I'll say it was a gross miscalculation to go flying off to Boleran Hall in the middle of the night."

"Again," Chloe added. She huffed. "You could at least have woken me and taken me with you this time."

"Or me," Shannon said. "It would have been best if

we'd all gone together. That way, you wouldn't have been so devilishly importuned by that blackguard."

Colleen was still wrapped up in her memories, but her gaze slowly focused as she turned to Shannon. "No, I mean I think I might have been mistaken about Benedict all along."

"Benedict?" both Shannon and Chloe asked in unison.

Colleen nodded slowly. A fond smile spread across her face, and her heart felt too big for her chest. A moment later, it thudded to her feet. She let out a breath and buried her face in her hands.

"The man has always been so perfectly vile to me," she lamented. "Or so I thought. He antagonized me so whenever we encountered one another. He has always said such vexing things to me at balls and other events, and he treated me like a disobedient child when I was at his house." She paused, her expression shifting from irritated to despondent as she let go of her old frustration.

"But?" Shannon asked, resting a hand over Colleen's.

Colleen sighed. "But I'm beginning to wonder if his teasing was not some sort of expression of fondness. Perhaps it was a way for him to indicate that he found me a worthy adversary."

Shannon and Chloe nodded consideringly.

"I've always assumed he was a boor and a blackguard, but to be fair, he did treat me with far more kindness than I should have expected, as an interloper in his house, last night and before," Colleen went on.

Chloe gasped. "No, Colleen, you aren't saying...." She clapped a hand to her mouth.

Colleen glanced mournfully at her. "You didn't hear the things he said to Fergus just now. He has done a great kindness for a farmer who was robbed by the Murphy gang. And he has treated his servants with magnanimity that very few employers would." She would leave out the details. She wasn't sure if she would know how to explain it, even if she chose to share. "And he's helping Cousin Cailean with his glider, and storing money for him, and who knows what other acts of kindness he is engaged in where others are concerned." Once she was started, the words flowed out at a rapid pace. "And he speaks so kindly of his deceased wife, even though he admits that it was not a love match." She gulped. "He said such kind things to Fergus about me just now," she finished in a near whisper.

"This cannot be," Shannon said gravely, her eyes wide.

"You aren't saying that you actually *like* the man now, are you?" Chloe asked.

"Surely not," Shannon added. "The fabric of the Universe would be ripped in two if Colleen suddenly decided to like Lord Boleran. Great earthquakes would have shaken us to our bones and the stars would have fallen."

"After detesting the man for so long," Chloe said.

"It simply cannot be."

Colleen looked one way, then the other, then back

again, as if observing a tennis match, as her sisters spoke. An ironic sort of misery welled up within her as they did. It grew so powerful and so large that she blurted, "I think I love him," interrupting the volley of words.

Both Shannon and Chloe gasped, pressing hands to their chests and leaning away from her.

"What did he do to you last night?" Chloe asked in a whisper.

"I think I know," Shannon answered with dread. "And I had no idea the act could produce such powerful effects."

Colleen laughed. The shift in her mood from dour to giddy happened so fast that it left her reeling. Laughter continued to burst out of her to the point where she had to stifle it with a hand to her mouth. "This is all completely and absolutely ridiculous," she said, tears stinging at her eyes. Whether they were tears of amusement or those of frustration—both for the awkward situation Benedict had put her in and for her own foolishness —was difficult to tell.

"What are you going to do about it all?" Shannon asked at last. "Does Lord Boleran know that you love him?"

"No." Colleen shook her head. "I'm only just realizing it myself." And if she were honest with herself, she had loved him for quite some time. At least, she'd been enamored of him. On some level. Otherwise, why would she have stayed so willingly at his house under such scandalous circumstances? Why would she have been so eager to stroke and touch him the first night, when he'd deliberately baited her? And why would she rush back to his house in the middle of the night under a frivolous excuse, and then stayed once she was caught?

She could only conclude that it was all exactly as Benedict had teased her it was. She wanted to be with him, at Boleran Hall, more than she wanted to be at home with her family.

"This is alarming indeed," she said, her gaze losing focus as she sank into the sofa.

"Well, it is not as alarming as it could be," Chloe pointed out. "You are already engaged to marry him, after all. So you don't need to worry about that."

"She does have a point," Shannon said. "From the sound of things at breakfast, that wedding will take place very soon."

"What is his sun sign, do you suppose?" Chloe asked with a serious frown. "He seems like a Capricorn to me. Perhaps that would help us to determine what you should do next."

"What I should do next," Colleen said, sitting straight again, "is follow the advice that Fergus gave Benedict just now."

Shannon and Chloe exchanged looks. "What advice was that?" Shannon asked.

Colleen bit her lip for a moment as ideas began to flood her. "He advised Benedict to treat me as an equal. At least, that was the gist of his advice. And to speak to me, to consult me on matters of importance."

Shannon tilted her head to the side in consideration. "Yes, I can see how that would be essential in a marital relationship."

Colleen stood suddenly. "So that is exactly what I am going to do."

Chloe blinked in confusion. "Consult with Lord Boleran on a matter of importance?"

"Precisely." Colleen's heart beat faster and faster, and she started to pace as her thoughts turned toward the Murphy gang. That seemed to be Benedict's foremost concern, other than the way she'd stumbled her way into forcing an engagement between the two of them.

She nearly missed a step in her pacing. Dear heavens, she had been the one to trap him into marriage, not the other way around. If she had simply stayed at home—or run from the barn the way Chloe had—he never would have found himself engaged to her. Had Benedict had any intention of remarrying? Had he had his eye on another, finer lady?

She shook her head and resumed her pacing. That was water under the bridge now. She had other things to focus on.

"Benedict will still have Cousin Cailean's money at Boleran Hall for a few more days or weeks," she said, thinking aloud.

"Cousin Cailean's money?" Chloe exchanged a confused look with Shannon. "I thought he was housing Cailean's glider, the dragon."

"I suppose the money is the dragon's hoard?" Shannon said, her face lighting with amusement.

Colleen gasped. That was all it took. One silly, flippant comment, and an entire plan formed in her mind. Catching the Murphy gang would be easy. If they did things like preyed on farmers returning from livestock sales, they wouldn't be able to resist what might seem to them like easy pickings. All she needed to do was form her plan fully, then explain it to Benedict.

"I need to work this plan out," she said, turning and heading toward the door. "And then I need to tell Benedict."

"I believe he is still here, speaking with Fergus," Shannon pointed out.

Colleen wasn't certain if he was or if he'd left. She rather thought he'd left. The sisters' parlor wasn't directly in the path Benedict would have taken from Fergus's study to the front door, so they wouldn't have seen him leave. But there was more to it than that.

"I need to call on him properly," she said, tilting her chin up. "So that he knows I am serious and not some silly child who creeps about other people's houses in the middle of the night."

Because that was all Benedict would be able to see of her. That was the only side of herself she'd shown him. But there was so much more to her than the anxious frivolity of a young woman who feared being constricted and diminished by the role life had for women. She wouldn't be that young woman for much longer. She would be Benedict's marchioness, and it was high time she started to act like it.

She rushed upstairs and pored through her wardrobe, searching for a day gown that would convey the image she wanted to present. Once she decided on that, she brushed and styled her hair, even finding a fetching hat to perch atop her hairstyle. Chloe and Shannon joined her after her preparations had already begun, and by the time they finished, Colleen looked as grand as she'd ever looked.

"If you are planning to call on Lord Boleran properly," Shannon said as they headed down to the front hall, "you should go with a chaperone."

"I should," Colleen admitted. "But given the nature of this visit, a chaperone is one propriety I'll have to forego. Besides," she added, "I overheard Benedict say something about expecting Cousin Cailean at his house this afternoon. If he is there, that will be good enough for me."

For a change, Colleen didn't ride her bicycle across the fields and byways to Boleran Hall. She didn't think she could have, with her current appearance. She took one of Fergus's carriages. Even Lady Coyle would have approved.

"Lady Colleen O'Shea, my lord," Mr. Conyers introduced her properly and everything, once she arrived at the house.

Sure enough, Benedict was taking tea and chatting about something with Cousin Cailean as she swept into the room, shoulders back, chin up, hair balanced atop her head, looking every bit the part she was supposed to play. She must have been quite a sight as well, because both Benedict and Cousin Cailean dropped their conversation —and their jaws—and stood to greet her.

"Good heavens, Colleen," Cailean blurted. "I've never seen you looking so...so grown up."

"But of course she looks grown up," Benedict said, his eyes flashing with a heated sort of pride that made Colleen feel far too flattered for her own good. "She is the future marchioness, after all."

Colleen wanted to shout in triumph. Benedict was fooled. That was to say, her attempt at nobility had hit its mark. She kept her face smooth and serene as she walked deeper into the room, though.

"Good afternoon, Cousin Cailean, Lord Boleran," she said, trying to sound more refined as well as look it. "I have come to discuss a matter of great importance with you, my lord." She turned to Benedict, wasting no time. "You see, I have an idea for how the Murphy gang might be thwarted."

Benedict's shock at her statement was gratifying. It was clear as day to Colleen the Murphy gang was the very last thing he thought she might want to talk about. She burned with curiosity to see if he would take Fergus's advice or if she had been right in her assessment of him as an overbearing boor. To her surprise, she desperately hoped it wasn't the latter.

Benedict glanced to Cailean. "Would you mind giving me and my fiancée a moment alone?"

Colleen's brow rose. Now who was being the improper one?

"Certainly." Cailean could hardly contain his grin as he glanced between the two of them. "I believe I'll take a walk down to the barn to visit my dragon."

"Tell the beast I say hello," Colleen said as he walked past her.

Cailean's head snapped back to her. He looked both amused and impressed, and laughed as he walked out of the room.

"I suppose I should have asked him to stay," Colleen said, taking the reins of the conversation once Cailean was gone, "seeing as it is his money I wish to use as bait to catch the Murphy gang."

Benedict's stunned and delighted look evened out to a curious look. "Don't tell me you have a brilliant and fool-proof plan, like Quigley and Parsons did." Benedict stepped slowly closer to her.

Colleen caught her breath at the way he looked at her as he drew closer. His gaze was intoxicating. Now that she knew what Benedict was capable of in terms of bringing both of them intense pleasure, she knew exactly what a look like that was all about. The man didn't think he could actually seduce her in the middle of the afternoon, did he? And he had implied that *she* was the wild and wicked one.

But then, she supposed, Benedict's behavior now—or

at least the suggestion of how he might behave—was proof that the two of them were well suited. No matter what, as Chloe would suggest, their star signs were.

"Unlike Mr. Quigley and Mr. Parsons's plan," Colleen began, moving away from him but giving him a look as heated as his own over her shoulder, "mine actually stands a chance of succeeding."

"Is that so?" Benedict followed her.

Colleen continued to move around the perimeter of the room. She rather enjoyed the feeling that he was chasing her. Or perhaps that she was leading the chase. "The Murphy gang takes advantage of easy money," she said, reflecting his words to Fergus without admitting she'd eavesdropped on the entire conversation. "Therefore, to catch them, all that is needed is to lure them into what they think is a simple theft."

Benedict paused in their slow chase, blinking as he thought about her words. "I'm listening," he said when the silence stretched on. Colleen wondered if his comment was born out of Fergus's advice about how to interact with a wife.

"Evidently, after last night at least, the Murphy gang knows that you are housing Cailean's money. They know it," Colleen pointed out. "And since they now know that you know that they know, they wouldn't be at all surprised if you attempted to move the money to a bank as swiftly as possible."

"But your cousin's bank cannot spare the proper sort of wagon and guards to come collect it," Benedict said.

Colleen's heart beat harder in her chest. On the surface, it was a simple statement, completely innocuous. But in reality, those words contained details about the situation that Colleen didn't think Benedict would ever have shared with her before. He was making an effort. He was attempting to take Fergus's advice and deal with her fairly, to treat her as an equal.

"You wouldn't need to actually take the money to a bank," Colleen went on. "You wouldn't actually need to remove it from the house at all. Just make them believe you had moved it. Make them believe you had put it somewhere easy for them to reach. Like a certain barn, guarded by a certain dragon."

Benedict laughed, and all of Colleen's high hopes started to tumble down. "Not even the Murphy gang would believe Cailean or I would be foolish enough to store that sum of money in a barn with a glider."

Colleen fought the frustration that crept down her spine. "Wouldn't they?" She shrugged. "Because when Chloe and I ran into scouts from the gang the other night, when we were on our mission to discover what the dragon was, they didn't seem that bright."

Benedict's expression was alarmed. "You encountered the Murphy gang? Are you all right? Why didn't you inform me of their presence?" He stepped quickly into her, clasping her arms and holding her close, as if he could protect her.

Colleen laughed. "That was days ago. Or nights, rather. And I'm not entirely certain that's who we encountered. But it seems to make sense." She paused. "I had entirely forgotten about those men, to be honest. You gave me other things to remember about that night." She sent him a sultry look for good measure.

"Yes, I suppose I did," he admitted. His eyes grew heated as he studied her.

Colleen could feel her thoughts scatter. She had to finish the mission she'd come on so that she could test just how determined Benedict was to be a good husband to her.

"I propose that we spread the word that Cailean's money is being moved to the barn. I further propose that we pretend as though both the money and the glider will be moved back to Cailean's estate after dark. Let word of the transfer slip at the pub or some such. Then, when we've said the transfer will happen, we'll hide in the barn, along with some police officers, and catch the Murphy gang in the act."

Benedict stared at her, long and hard. She could see the conflict behind his eyes as he weighed her plan. If her guess was right, he was debating whether to indulge her, as Fergus had suggested, or whether to dismiss the whole thing as silly, to dismiss *her* as silly. So much rode on the decision he was trying to make that Colleen could hardly breathe as she waited for his answer.

She decided to push him by saying, "I believe I was wrong about you, Benedict."

"Wrong?" His brow inched up as his focus returned to her.

"I thought you were a selfish, arrogant blackguard." She rested her hands on his chest. "But it has come to my attention that you care a great deal more for people than I first thought. You are a good man," she admitted, glancing at her hands on his broad chest instead of into his eyes for a moment. "I'm sorry that I rushed to such unkind conclusions about you." She looked up, meeting his eyes. "You are kinder than I thought you were."

He let out a breath, sliding his hands around her waist and pulling her closer. "And you are far cleverer than I assumed," he said, bringing his mouth to hers. "You know full well that if you compliment me like that, I will give in to whatever mad-capped plan you wish to try."

Colleen laughed in her throat. So he knew she'd been manipulating him with her charm after all. Strangely enough, knowing he had her number made her adore him even more. It had her ready and eager as he slanted his mouth over hers, kissing her with an all-encompassing passion that lifted her heart right out of her chest. But the kiss was different from the one they'd shared in the hallway that first night she'd snuck through his house. That kiss had been designed to prove a point of his dominance. This one cast them as equals, giving and taking from each other with a whole new level of understanding and need. She could have kissed him like that for hours.

"All right," he sighed at last, rocking back, but not letting her go. "We'll give your cunning scheme a go."

"Really?" Her eyes snapped wide. "Do you mean it? You'll really give my plan a chance?"

Benedict laughed. "I don't see that I have any choice. You'll make my life miserable if I don't."

Colleen smiled, throwing herself into Benedict's arms. If all else failed, at least she now knew Benedict could be taught.

CHAPTER 11

By the next evening, Benedict was seriously beginning to question why he was being so astoundingly indulgent in letting Colleen execute her mad plan to capture the Murphy gang in his barn.

"No, no, the decoy chest should go in the glider's seat," she ordered Officer McPhee as the man attempted to move it from the glider.

"Begging your pardon, my lady," the skeptical officer said, "but isn't there a danger that the Murphys will damage Lord Dervock's glider when they attempt to make off with the loot?"

Benedict—who stood to the side, watching Colleen and the trio of officers from Ballymena setting up their trap, along with Parsons and Quigley—crossed his arms and covered his wry smile with one hand. He should have warned the officer about second-guessing Colleen's plot. Granted, he should have put his foot down and prevented the entire entrapment event from happening. But Fergus's words had rung in his head almost constantly since the other afternoon. Treat Colleen as an equal. Listen to her, and make her feel as though she is a part of things. He'd extrapolated that last bit from Fergus's overall advice, but he was certain his soon-to-be brother-in-law would approve.

"If we all play our parts well," Colleen countered Officer McPhee, "the Murphy gang members will never get close enough to the glider to cause any damage. But they need to see that the chest is being stored here, in the barn. That's the rumor we circulated at The Hangman Pub in Ballymena."

"This whole thing is bally-something," Officer McPhee's assistant, Johnston, muttered.

Benedict gave the young man a stern look that was just enough to silence him. Granted, he agreed the whole endeavor was ridiculous. He also thought it was unlikely to actually succeed. Even though the officers were in plain clothes, milling about the barn as though they were investors, speculating about the glider, and even though the plan was for them to make a show of leaving and to wait in the dark at some distance from the barn until the Murphy gang showed up, Benedict couldn't imagine that a band of thieves that had been so successful in the past would be moronic enough to fall for such a blatantly obvious ploy.

But to be honest, he was just as moronic for allowing it to go forward.

"Perfect," Colleen said with a wide smile as Parsons and Quigley finished hanging a series of fishing nets above one of the glider's wings. "Now, just make certain that when one or more of the Murphys trips that wire you've set up in the hay, the nets fall on them so that they cannot get away."

"Yes, my lady," Parsons said, then grinned at Quigley. The two young men were having a grand time carrying out Colleen's plans. Benedict was certain they'd have a grand time polishing boots at this point, after the conversation he'd had with the two of them that morning, explaining why he wouldn't be sacking them as long as they were discreet.

"Oh, here, you're doing it wrong." Colleen picked up her skirts and traipsed across the straw-strewn barn floor to the side where Parsons and Quigley were working. Benedict raised his brow in surprise as she picked up her skirts and bent to gather an armful of the dirty straw. She was dressed for an evening out, which was part of the ploy. Any other woman would have balked at the idea of mussing her gown. "You need to make certain it's fully concealed." She dumped an armful of straw over the taut wire Parsons had set up.

Officer McPhee inched closer to Benedict, standing by his side and leaning in to mutter, "Is she like this all the time, my lord?"

"She is," Benedict said, watching Colleen and smiling. A proud, warm feeling spread through his chest. Most fine ladies he knew wouldn't deign to soil their gloves to help those less fortunate than themselves by catching thieves in the act. Colleen might have been wildly unconventional and astoundingly improper, but her heart was in the right place.

"It's all a bit daft, though," McPhee went on.

Benedict turned to frown at the man, causing him to blanch. "That is my future marchioness you are referring to," he said in a commanding voice.

"I—er—that is—begging your pardon, my lord," McPhee stammered. He hesitated, then said, "But you must admit, it is a wee bit strange."

"More than a wee bit," Benedict laughed. He let out a breath and thumped the officer on the back. "I'm merely trying to prove a point to the lady."

"And that point is?" McPhee asked, looking highly suspicious.

That he thought Colleen was wonderful, in spite of her eccentricities? That he wanted a happy wife, which required a gesture to prove that he would never stifle her imagination or her impulse to take action about things? That he loved her?

Benedict drew in a sharp breath at that last realization. He loved Colleen. Actually loved her, not just desired her. His feelings for her were more than just amusement or passing fondness. He loved her with his whole heart. Why else would he risk making himself look like a mad fool in front of his staff and officers from Ballymena?

"Are you married, McPhee?" he asked the officer.

"Er, no, my lord," McPhee answered. "But I do have my eye on a lovely young thing in the village where I was born."

Benedict thumped McPhee's back again. "Then you'll soon understand the lengths a man will go to when he's in love."

McPhee's mouth pulled into a lopsided grin. "If you say so, my lord."

Benedict nodded and stepped toward the glider, where Colleen had climbed up on a small ladder in her evening gown and was showing Parsons and Quigley how to fasten the fishing net properly.

"You must do it this way," she insisted, "so that it will not be visible in the dark."

"Whatever you say, my lady," Quigley agreed, glancing up at Colleen in adoration.

Benedict rolled his eyes. There was no telling what sort of mischief Colleen would be able to get up to as the marchioness if she had the first footman and his valet in her thrall. The two men would aid and abet her in just about any plot she might have in the future.

"Are we ready to put the plan in motion?" he asked, clasping his hands around Colleen's waist and removing her from the ladder. He had a feeling his fiancée would spend all evening setting the trap and forgetting about springing it if given half a chance. "It's already twilight, and this entire farce requires us to be ready at darkness."

"Then we'd better set the bait," Colleen said, a sparkling light in her eyes.

Benedict was slow to let go of her. It felt natural to have her in his arms and to hold her against him. It felt natural to do other things as well, but with five other men crowding around them, he wouldn't dare. Once he got rid of the officers and his staff, however....

"Now," Colleen said, pulling away from him—albeit reluctantly—and facing her henchmen, "Mr. Quigley and Mr. Parsons, are you prepared to masquerade as Lord Boleran and I and to take the carriage off the property?"

"We are, my lady," Parsons and Quigley answered in unison.

Colleen nodded approvingly at them. "Officer McPhee, are you and your men ready to station your-selves outside of the barn, nearby, and to answer our call when the Murphy gang arrives?"

McPhee sighed. "I suppose, my lady."

Colleen looked tempted to scold the man for lack of enthusiasm.

"Carry on, then," Benedict said, sending McPhee an amused warning look.

McPhee took the meaning as Benedict intended it and gestured to his men to follow him out of the barn. He caught a bit of muttering about madness and indulgent husbands as they left.

"That just leaves our part in this whole thing." Colleen turned to Benedict with a broad smile.

"Come on, then, my lady." Benedict held out a hand to her.

They left the barn, taking all the lanterns with them

and leaving the building in darkness, then crossed to the stable, which stood a bit farther up the drive toward the house. Benedict noted Colleen's bicycle leaning up against the outside of the barn wall in the dim light. A twist of dread filled his gut. The presence of that contraption could only mean she had something additional planned that he probably wasn't going to like.

"This is exciting, isn't it?" She practically danced as they approached Benedict's finest carriage, which was parked unusually close to the stable door. "It's exactly like some of the novels I enjoy reading, all subterfuge and danger in the middle of the night."

Benedict fought to keep his smile from being too indulgent. "Just like a novel," he agreed.

And he meant it. Just like a novel in that the whole thing was a fiction. He had no doubt in his mind that their evening was about to pass in uneventful disappointment. Not that he minded. He had plans of his own for the long middle part of Colleen's detailed scheme. Plans that he would be able to implement in no time at all.

"Now, make a show of handing me into the carriage," Colleen whispered as they approached the vehicle. "Make sure anyone watching knows we're going out."

Benedict sighed, feeling ridiculous, and said in a booming voice, "I trust your brother and sisters will be happy to see us this evening when we arrive at Dunegard Castle for supper."

"Yes, yes, like that," Colleen whispered as she stepped into the carriage. In a much louder voice, she said, "I do hope you stay all night. I think your house will be perfectly safe without you in it and with most of the servants taking the night off." She giggled, then ducked inside the carriage.

Benedict rolled his eyes and followed her in. Neither of them took their seats, though. They climbed all the way through the carriage, getting out the other door and allowing Parsons and Quigley to climb in to replace them. Why Colleen's plan required the two young men to replace them instead of simply sending the carriage off empty was beyond Benedict. He figured the men hadn't pointed out the unnecessary action for reasons of their own. Indeed, if he'd been in their position, having a carriage all to themselves for the evening would be a boon.

"Hurry, hurry," Colleen whispered as they made their way through the stable and out the back door as the carriage sped off. "We need to take up our positions in the barn as quickly as possible so we can be ready when the Murphy gang makes their attempt."

Benedict smirked, allowing Colleen to grasp his hand and lead him out the back of the stable and across the yard to the back of the barn. She clearly enjoyed every second of sneaking through the grass, keeping to the shadows, and attempting to conceal the light cast by the lantern she held.

She cried out in victory as they crept through a tiny back door and into the barn. She'd prepared their perch behind a pile of crates and hay bales in the far corner, and once they were secluded there, in her theory, all they had to do was wait.

"This is perfect," she whispered, setting the lantern on a crate and turning down its flame until it was just a dull glow. "All we do now is bide our time. The Murphy gang won't be able to resist the carrot we are dangling in front of them. I'd wager they'll be here as soon as it is full dark."

"I'm sure they will," Benedict lied. "Now come here and wait with me."

He sat on the crates she had specifically picked out for him as they'd set up the barn, then drew her into his lap. Colleen let out a yelp of surprise as he lifted her legs over his and held her close, sliding his hand across her silk-encased side.

"I think I rather like your plan," he growled, bending toward her.

"Benedict," she whispered, giggling low in her throat. "The point of things is to be watchful, not to become... distracted." Her last word was issued on a sigh as Benedict nibbled on her neck.

"Surely, the nefarious Murphys won't be making any attempts to steal the dragon's hoard immediately," he argued, kissing his way up the line of her neck to her jaw. "We have a great deal of time to fill until their arrival." He spoke his last words while gazing intimately at her.

"Yes," she breathed, resting a hand on his arm and gazing back with just as much heat. "I suppose we do have some time to—"

He closed his mouth over hers in a searing kiss before she could finish. A laugh rumbled through him even as he melded his mouth with hers. Colleen was a delight in so many ways. He discovered ever new and ever more charming things about her every time they were together. And her kisses were becoming more delightful all the time as well. She was a quick learner, and as he teased his tongue against hers, she gave as good as she got.

"You are my treasure," he breathed between kisses. His hands roved her sides, and he wondered if there were a way to undress her. Although, truth be told, he didn't have to undress her to have his way with her. "You drive me to distraction and vex me at every turn, but in the very best way possible."

"Benedict." The way she sighed his name was all the encouragement he needed.

He lifted her, doing a clumsy job of adjusting the way he held her so that she straddled him. She seemed to catch on to what he wanted, though, and wriggled against him. Her movements managed to ignite him in all the right places. He'd already been well on his way to being aroused, but the friction of her eager body seeking his out was too much for him to deny.

"My darling Colleen," he groaned, tugging her dress off her shoulder and kissing the flesh he exposed. "You are the most beautiful thing I've ever seen."

"Oh, my, but that feels nice," she gasped as he nipped her neck and cupped one of her breasts.

Benedict wanted more than nice. He shifted again,

pulling at her skirts until he had them bunched around her waist. As her long, stocking-clad legs were freed, he moved them farther apart and up over his hips. When that was done, he reached for the fastenings of his trousers.

She was one step ahead of him, panting restlessly and swatting his hands away so that she could finish undoing them. He groaned shamelessly as she freed his cock and stroked his aching length eagerly.

"We are so wicked," she laughed, glancing into his eyes. "I adore this."

"I adore you," he gasped in return. "I love you, Colleen." The confession burst out of him before he could stop it.

Colleen's entire face lit up. "I love you too," she said, as though surprised they felt the same way about each other.

Benedict wanted to launch into a grand and glorious speech that would make the poets weep and jealous young maidens sigh. He wanted to, but words completely escaped him. Instead, he teased his hands between her thighs, parting the soft fabric of her drawers to find her hot, wet sex, and then sheathed himself in her to the hilt.

"Oh!" Colleen cried out, tilting her head back. "I didn't know we could—"

Her words turned into sighs as Benedict bucked his hips hard and fast into her. Sense told him he should be careful, but desire and love wouldn't let him. He held Colleen around the waist, jerking into her for all he was worth...until he realized that she had picked up on their rhythm and was moving on him. She'd taken complete control and rode him as if she'd been born for it.

That was enough to set Benedict over the edge. He tilted his head back, his impassioned sounds turning into curses that a lady like Colleen most definitely shouldn't hear, until his entire body and soul focused into one white-hot flash of pleasure as—

A massive crash sounded from the barn just as Benedict came hard. Colleen let out a cry, but whether from her own orgasm or from shock, it was impossible to tell. The crash from the barn was followed by a few more. That wasn't all. Deep but indistinct shouts and curses that were even ruder than Benedict's own echoed in the barn. Faint light, as if from more lanterns, illuminated the rafters above them.

Colleen struggled off of Benedict with a yelp. Benedict gasped and winced at the clumsy, and slightly painful, way he disengaged from her as a result. Where he expected Colleen to be horrified or frightened at the very least, she appeared exultant.

"We have them!" she declared, pushing her skirts down and stumbling toward the lamp she'd discarded. She looked both comical and triumphant, flushed and gossamer with sweat from lovemaking as she leapt out of their concealed position. "They fell for it," she told him, as if she'd never had any doubt, before turning up the flame of her lamp and bouncing into the main part of the barn.

Thoroughly stunned and convinced he'd jettisoned his mind along with his seed when he'd come, Benedict fastened his trousers and pushed himself up after her.

"Stop right there, thieves!" Colleen shouted as Benedict leapt out of hiding to be by her side. "We've got you."

Benedict found himself face to face with five burly men in rough clothes, armed with clubs, knives, and pistols.

CHAPTER 12

*N*ever in all her life would Colleen have imagined that there was anything as wonderful as engaging in something as miraculous and wicked as joining with Benedict the way they were in a darkened barn. She was still fully dressed, which felt both bizarre and surprisingly good as she impaled herself on Benedict's staff. Why had no one told her that she was perfectly capable of controlling the movements necessary to—

Her thoughts ended at roughly that point, and the pleasure of her body accepting Benedict as he made the most wonderful sounds overtook her. He didn't seem to mind at all if she was the power behind their joining. In fact, the more she directed the movements, the more he seemed transported with bliss. Her own pleasure built within her, made better by the way she was able to shift slightly so that everything hit just as it should to—oh! Oh!

She was within inches of completion, gasping as she felt a warm spurt from Benedict, when the crash of her trap being set off jerked her out of the trance of pleasure and rocketed her into an entirely different sort of victory. Her plan had worked.

She stumbled back, noticing Benedict's wince and groan, but didn't have time to address it. Not when the thieves were there and might possibly get away. "We have them! They fell for it!" the words tumbled out of her mouth, expressing her surprise, as she grabbed for her lantern. She turned it up—although she noted the thieves had lanterns with them as well—then leapt out of her hiding place.

"Stop right there, thieves! We've got you."

Benedict gathered himself together enough to jump out by her side, but that wasn't what made her eyes pop wide and her heart drop to her stomach. She'd expected the same three, rather unimpressive men that she and Chloe had encountered days before, when they'd come to investigate the dragon. She did not expect five large and armed men.

The only saving grace she could see in the situation was that the five men were as startled to see her and Benedict as she was to see them.

"Shit!" the one who had ventured deepest into the barn shouted. "We've been had!"

"You said the barn would be empty," another hollered.

"It's just a girl and a nob," a third one said.

That last comment—perhaps coupled with the exhilaration Colleen felt from her activities with Benedict and being so close to climax without being allowed to indulge —sent a surge of energy through Colleen the likes of which she had never felt before.

"Surrender, you heathens!" she shouted, advancing on them. "Your days of wickedness and infamy are over."

"Shit!" the rude thief shouted again, backpedaling right into the tripwire Colleen had directed Mr. Parsons and Mr. Quigley to set up.

And, miracle of miracles, the trap worked.

To a degree.

The fishing nets arranged above Cailean's glider's wings tumbled down, covering the rude thief. The man's pistol went off, splitting the air with a deafening crack.

At the same time, Benedict shouted, "Get out of here!"

Colleen wasn't certain if it was the command in Benedict's voice, if the shock of finding the barn occupied was too much for the thieves, or if they somehow assumed the gunshot was somehow from Benedict and not one of their own, but the four thieves who weren't trapped by fishing nets turned tail and ran, shouting things like, "Run! Run!" or "I told you this was a bad idea!"

Colleen felt a momentary surge of triumph as she watched the villains scamper away into the night. That triumph felt flat a moment later as she realized they were getting away. She launched into motion, picking up her skirts and dashing around the thief who was thrashing under the fishing nets.

"You won't get away with this," she called after the thieves. They were easy to spot, as they all carried lanterns in their flight. "You will be brought to justice. Officer McPhee!"

She doubted the officer was within shouting distance, but that didn't stop her from taking matters into her own hands. Like one of the heroines of her novels, she dashed out of the barn and around the corner to where she'd left her bicycle earlier. Even though she was a woman, with her bicycle, she would be faster than the thieves. She could catch them.

It was much, much more difficult to ride a bicycle in an evening gown than it was in the plain skirt she usually wore for such an activity. Colleen had to gather her skirts clumsily around her waist as she pedaled into motion. It was surprisingly uncomfortable to ride after the activity she and Benedict had been engaged in as well. But she was determined to catch the thieves before they could get away.

So determined that she ignored Benedict's shout of, "Colleen, wait! What in blazes are you doing, you madwoman?"

Any irritation she might have felt at Benedict's epithet vanished a few minutes later when she managed to catch up to the four escaping thieves where the gravel drive of Boleran Hall met the road. Riding a bicycle did indeed prove to be an effective way to catch up with thieves—to catch up with them in the dark, by herself, far away from anyone with strength or a weapon who might be able to come to her aid.

"She's the one who set the trap," one of the thieves called out when they, too, realized Colleen was alone and defenseless.

"She'll fetch a pretty penny as well," another of the thieves said. "Lord Boleran will pay through the nose."

"Don't you dare," Colleen yelped. She slid off of the seat of her bicycle but kept the contraption between her legs, hoping it would act as a sort of shield—or at least a deterrent.

She was only partially right. The thieves each took a turn lunging at her, laughing and making rude sounds as they did. Colleen swatted at them as best she could, wishing she had a weapon of her own. The brutes were toying with her, she could tell. But how quickly would their teasing turn into genuine abuse?

The one silver lining her mind conjured up from the dangerous situation was that the thieves truly must not be that bright at all if they had actually fallen for her imaginative ploy, and if they were wasting time baiting her when they could be getting away.

"Old Ryan will be pleased as punch to see we've captured a nob lady as a hostage," one of the thieves laughed. He seemed to answer her speculations when he went on to say, "Now he'll take us seriously."

"Yeah, he'll give us the important heists now," another of the men seconded.

Colleen supposed she should be pleased that Old Ryan—whom she assumed was the leader of the Murphy gang—had insubordinate men in his circle. She would feel a lot more pleased about it if she were able to fight them off. Too soon, as she'd predicted, they grew tired of playing with her. The biggest of the lot finally reached in and scooped her clean off of her bicycle, dragging her to the grass by the side of the road.

Colleen screamed like she'd never screamed before, but followed that with an attempt to bash her knee into the man's groin. "Unhand me, you cur!" she shouted.

"Hold her down and get on with it," one of the men growled. "I want a turn with her."

Cold dread reached deep into Colleen, and for a moment, her strength faltered. She could try all she wanted, but she would never be strong enough to fight off four large men.

"Colleen!" Benedict's shout renewed her courage in an instant. His voice was accompanied by the sound of a galloping horse.

There was just enough light from the four thieves' lanterns for Colleen to make out Benedict riding toward them, bareback, on a black horse. The thieves shouted and started to scatter, but Benedict wasn't the only one riding to her rescue. Behind Benedict, Colleen could make out Officer McPhee and his assistants running forward, lanterns in their hands. Not only that, but Mr. Quigley and Mr. Parsons were charging up the road from where Colleen could now see the carriage was parked.

Once again, the two young men were in a state of undress, and this time the fighting hadn't even started.

"Stop them!" Officer McPhee shouted at the scattering members of the Murphy gang.

The man who had dragged Colleen off her bicycle and had her pinned was the slowest to react. Benedict reached him before he could stand fully and stumble away from Colleen, and she was certain in an instant the man would regret being so slow. Benedict grabbed him by the shirt and punched him with so much ferocity that the impact of his fist against the thief's face rang in the night. Benedict didn't stop there, he punched the man a few more times, until the blackguard stumbled back and spilled into a heap in the road. Benedict stared at him, teeth bared, fists balled, panting with fury.

It really was counter to everything Colleen believed about herself, her strength, a woman's place in the world, and how men should behave, but her heart beat faster at the idea that Benedict had ridden to her rescue and thrashed the man who had tried to harm her. She shouldn't have found his brutish behavior half as arousing as she did, but something about the sight of Benedict in full, protective glory had the parts of her that were already sore and tingling from earlier alive all over again.

She was snapped out of that invigorating thought by Mr. Parsons calling, "We have these two," farther down the road.

"This one isn't going anywhere either," one of Officer McPhee's assistants called out from the other direction.

"We've got them," Officer McPhee himself said. "I don't believe it, but we've actually got them. And I recognize this one. He's Paddy Murphy, Old Ryan's nephew."

The captured members of the Murphy gang groaned, and one even started crying, as they were gathered together.

"There's one more back outside of the barn," Benedict told Officer McPhee as he strode to help Colleen to her feet. "He was caught up in the nets, but I had the stableman tie him up tighter before giving chase."

As soon as Colleen was on her feet, Benedict crushed her to his chest. She was perfectly amenable to the gesture and threw her arms around him in return. "Thank God," she sighed, pressing her face against his neck.

"Were you frightened?" Benedict asked.

Colleen jerked back and frowned up at him. "Absolutely not," she insisted, though it was more than a little bit of a lie. "I knew you would rescue me."

Benedict eyed her disapprovingly, but that didn't last. He crushed her against him, then kissed her with a passion that was devilishly scandalous, considering how many men were nearby. Those men didn't seem to mind, though. In fact, Mr. Quigley and Mr. Parsons looked downright charmed by the gesture.

"We'll see that these men are taken to the jail in Ballymena," Officer McPhee said as the tension in the air began to subside. "My guess is that they'll all squeal like pigs and tell us everything we need to know about the location of every member of the Murphy gang."

"We will not," one of the thieves said.

"Oh, yes, you will," Officer McPhee said threateningly.

Colleen was certain Officer McPhee would be the one to have his way in the end. He and his assistants—with the help of Mr. Quigley and Mr. Parsons—rounded the four men up and marched them back onto the grounds of Boleran Hall, where Colleen figured the officers had a wagon waiting. Benedict loosened his hold on Colleen long enough for the two of them to gather Colleen's bicycle and the horse Benedict had ridden to her rescue and to walk them back up the gravel drive to the stable.

"I suppose I should return to Dunegard Castle and explain to Fergus what happened tonight," Colleen said with a frown once the stableman had Benedict's horse back in its stall.

"You will do no such thing," Benedict told her. He stepped closer to her, glowering over her. "I let you get away with far too much nonsense this evening. I will be honest and tell you I never expected this mad-capped plan of yours to work."

"But it did," Colleen interrupted, grinning coyly at him.

Benedict pressed his lips shut, huffing though his nose. "By pure coincidence," he said. "I was willing to indulge you because I have no wish to crush that wild and indomitable spirit within you."

"Why, Benedict. How very kind of you," Colleen said, unable to suppress a giggle. It didn't matter that her plan worked. It didn't even matter if it was a good plan. Benedict had gone along with it because he wanted her to be happy. That meant everything to her.

Benedict was clearly irritated by the whole thing, though. At least, the spark in his eyes might have been irritation. It might have been something else as well, something that made her breath catch in her throat.

"We're going back to the house," he said, surprising her by sweeping her into his arms. Colleen yelped, but that sound was followed by laughter as he marched toward the house with her. "We're going to have Mrs. Ferrer draw us a bath."

"Us?" Colleen asked, her stomach fluttering wildly.

"My tub is big enough for two," Benedict told her, his tone half warning, half promise. "And once we're clean, we are going to go to bed and finish what we started in the barn."

"My lord," Colleen said with exaggerated formality, "I believe you *did* finish what you started in the barn."

He arched one eyebrow as he glanced to her. "And did you?"

"Well, no, but—"

"Then don't argue with me, madwoman."

Colleen burst into another round of laughter. She should have been far more scandalized by her actions.

She should have been appalled by the way Benedict manhandled her all the way through the house and during their bath. He insisted on scrubbing her as though she were a wriggling and disobedient child in his care.

Well, not quite like a child at all. There were far too many kisses for her to be a child, and he seemed particularly intent on making certain her breasts and tender areas were rubbed thoroughly clean. Not that she minded. The warm water of the tub was a revelation that only added to the wealth of sensation sending her to new heights of arousal.

By the time Benedict carried her from the washroom across the hall to his bedchamber and dumped her unceremoniously on his bed, Colleen was relaxed and giddy and throbbing with expectation. Better still, Benedict seemed to have no qualms at all about his naked and aroused state, or about the way she ran her hands over his body, learning him and exciting herself as she did.

"You realize this is all highly improper, my lord," she said as he nestled between her legs, bending down to nip her neck and fondle one of her breasts. "If Lady Coyle could see the two of us as we are now, she would insist on having the wedding tomorrow."

"Lady Coyle be damned," Benedict said in a low, rumbling voice that made Colleen want to wriggle right out of her skin.

She expected him to follow that up with another colorful invective, but instead, he kissed his way from her neck, over her breasts, and down the plane of her stomach. Each new area of her that he explored hitched her breath tighter in her lungs. She'd never imagined being at a man's mercy could make her feel so incredible. If this was the sort of pleasure she could be expected to feel every time the two of them were together, then perhaps married life wasn't such a curse after—

Her thought ended in a long, indulgent cry as Benedict tugged her legs wide apart, then brought his mouth over that part of her that was already dripping and aching for him. The forcefulness of the way he held her wide open combined with the sweetness of his mouth on her had Colleen moaning and gasping as she tried to writhe against him. Being held still was even better than being able to move, though. She settled for threading her fingers through Benedict's wet hair and holding on tight as he licked and suckled and explored her with his tongue.

She could have been happy letting him continue his ministrations forever, but her body burst into throbbing orgasm all too soon. It was so powerful that she cried out and clenched her hands hard in his hair as tremors passed through her entire body. He made her feel so good that she thought she might lose her mind.

That was only half of it. Moments later, before her climax had stopped, he shifted to slide himself deep inside of her. Colleen's moaning cries were renewed as he thrust into her, taking for himself what he'd just given her. She loved the feel of him filling and stretching her, even to the point where she knew she would be damnably sore in the morning. She loved the ferocity of the way he claimed her and the way they seemed to melt into each other. And she loved the ripping cry that accompanied him spilling himself inside of her, regardless of the risk it might bring several weeks down the road. They were to be married anyhow, and as far as she was concerned, the sooner the better.

At last, when both of their energy was spent and they lay, panting and overheated, together, Colleen let herself relax.

"Well, my lord," she gasped as she caught her breath. "That was quite an evening, was it not?"

"You will be the death of me, Colleen," Benedict said, flopping to his back and tucking her against him.

"Yes," she agreed, nestling contentedly against him and throwing an arm and a leg over his body. "But you will die happy."

He laughed, the sound encompassing her and making her feel as though all would be right in the world from thenceforth.

"I love you, you little minx," he said.

"And I love you too."

EPILOGUE

o one questioned why the Marquess of Boleran would marry Lady Colleen O'Shea within just a few short weeks of the couple announcing their engagement. No one questioned it, because they were all quite certain impropriety and scandal were behind the whole thing. But rather than finding herself shunned from polite social gatherings and cast off from the higher circles of society in the Ascendency, Colleen found herself right at its center. For it was well known that she was responsible for the downfall of the Murphy gang.

"When I heard, I simply couldn't believe it," Lady Toome said after congratulating Colleen and Benedict during the reception after their wedding. "To think that a lady could outwit a gang of thieves in such a manner. Can you believe it, Lord Blackburn?" she asked, turning to the man who had been a guest at her husband's house for the last few months.

"I suppose I shall have to believe it," Lord Blackburn said. "And I am highly impressed that a woman could accomplish such a feat." He smiled, then went on with a laugh, "Do you have any sisters, Lady Boleran?"

They would probably never forgive her for it, but Colleen answered, "In fact, I have two unmarried sisters, your grace." She turned, pointing to where Shannon and Chloe stood near the refreshment table.

Chloe was just stuffing her mouth with an overlarge slice of wedding cake when Lord Blackburn smiled at her. She proceeded to gasp, then choke on the cake.

"That is my sister, Chloe," Colleen informed him. "Perhaps you could help her with a glass of something to stop that cough?" Colleen paused, then went on with, "But only if you're a Leo, an Aquarius, or an Aries."

Lord Blackburn blinked. "I beg your pardon."

"She is teasing you, your grace," Lady Toome laughed. "Perhaps you should go help the young lady."

Lady Toome pushed Lord Blackburn toward the refreshment table, where Chloe was still coughing as Shannon slapped her back. She sent Colleen a worried look over her shoulder as they left, as if wondering whether it was a good idea to be friends with Colleen after all.

Colleen, for her part, just laughed. "I do so enjoy watching fellow members of the aristocracy as they attempt to reconcile their moral outrage with their need to look as though they approve of the right people."

"What do you think she would say if she knew the next marquess will be born perhaps seven months after the wedding?" Benedict whispered in Colleen's ear.

"Or the next marchioness," Colleen told him with one raised eyebrow, resting a hand covertly on her stomach.

Benedict laughed. "Inheritance doesn't work that way, my darling."

"Well, it should," Colleen said, tilting her chin up as she leaned into Benedict's side. "Either way, I shall weather the storm of moral outrage that is to come gladly."

"As will I," Benedict said, sliding an arm around her waist. The two of them watched their wedding guests together, but their attention ended up focused on Lord Blackburn as he attempted to help Chloe recover from breathing cake. Fergus was nearby, observing the interaction from his wheelchair with a sly look in his one eye. "Your sister isn't going to forgive you for setting up your brother's next marriage trap," Benedict said.

"Perhaps not, but Lord Blackburn is a duke. I think even Chloe would put aside her reservations about marriage for a man like him."

Benedict hummed. "That begs the question, though. Why would an English duke put aside whatever reservations he might have to pursue the youngest sister of an Irish earl?"

"Oh!" Colleen perked up. "I don't know. What a delicious mystery. I'm certain he has some sort of skeleton in his closet. Just like a gothic novel. I wonder what it could be."

Benedict laughed. "I do love you, you know," he said, turning her in his arms so that he could smile down at her.

"And I think it is now well established that, in spite of my earlier protestations, I adore you as well, my marquess."

She lifted to her toes and kissed him soundly, not caring who saw them or what they thought.

§.

I hope you've enjoyed Colleen and Benedict's story! But what about Chloe and the mysterious Duke of Blackburn? What is an English duke doing in Ireland looking for a bride, and why would he possibly be content with Lady Chloe O'Shea? Maybe the answer is written in the stars? Or maybe you'll be able to find out next in *All About That Duke, available for preorder now*!

If you enjoyed this book and would like to hear more from me, please sign up for my newsletter! When you sign up, you'll get a free, full-length novella, *A Passionate Deception*. Victorian identity theft has never been so exciting in this story of hope, tricks, and starting over. Part of my West Meets East series, *A Passionate Deception* can be read as a stand-alone. Pick up your free copy today by signing up to receive my newsletter (which I only send out when I have a new release)!

Sign up here: http://eepurl.com/cbaVMH

ARE YOU ON SOCIAL MEDIA? I AM! COME AND JOIN the fun on Facebook: http://www. facebook.com/merryfarmerreaders

I'M ALSO A HUGE FAN OF INSTAGRAM AND POST LOTS of original content there: https://www. instagram.com/merryfarmer/

Click here for a complete list of other works by Merry Farmer.

ABOUT THE AUTHOR

I hope you have enjoyed *If You Wannabe My Marquess*. If you'd like to be the first to learn about when new books in the series come out and more, please sign up for my newsletter here: http://eepurl.com/cbaVMH And remember, Read it, Review it, Share it! For a complete list of works by Merry Farmer with links, please visit http://wp.me/P5ttjb-14F.

Merry Farmer is an award-winning novelist who lives in suburban Philadelphia with her cats, Torpedo, her grumpy old man, and Justine, her hyperactive new baby. She has been writing since she was ten years old and realized one day that she didn't have to wait for the teacher to assign a creative writing project to write something. It was the best day of her life. She then went on to earn not one but two degrees in History so that she would always have something to write about. Her books have reached the Top 100 at Amazon, iBooks, and Barnes & Noble, and have been named finalists in the prestigious RONE and Rom Com Reader's Crown awards.

ACKNOWLEDGMENTS

I owe a huge debt of gratitude to my awesome beta-readers, Caroline Lee and Jolene Stewart, for their suggestions and advice. And double thanks to Julie Tague, for being a truly excellent editor and to Cindy Jackson for being an awesome assistant!

Click here for a complete list of other works by Merry Farmer.

Printed in Great Britain
by Amazon

69659330R00108